Grandmother Detective

David Evans

Table of Contents

Chapter 1 The Neighbors 14

Chapter 2 Housework.....................25

Chapter 3 The Mop 36

Chapter 4 Train Ride 47

Chapter 5 The Talk 58

Chapter 6 Discomfort 68

Chapter 7 Frustration 79

Chapter 8 Mr Mittens 90

Chapter 9 Bonding 101

Chapter 10 The Officer 119

Chapter 11 Questions 130

Chapter 12 Situation 142

Chapter 13 Hospital 153

Chapter 14 Pests 165

Chapter 15 Mr Hinkle 176

Chapter 16 Effort 187

Chapter 17 It Begins 205

Chapter 18 Mission 218

Two years ago, the FBI hired Bernice, who's an eighty-year-old grandmother. Bernice has helped the FBI catch even the most dangerous of convicts.

She's good at sneaking around and finding evidence, she's been working for the FBI for going on three years now. However, today they gave her a raise.

She figured out a century-long case, nobody could ever figure out the case. Bernice worked on the case for two months, she found many pieces of evidence.

She makes sure that she finds all the finger prints at the crime scene, she doesn't have a partner, and likes to do all the work by herself.

Bernice wears a large gray hat, white gloves. When her hips are hurting her she takes her cane with her, but as of lately she hasn't needed her cane. She likes to wear her all black running suit, she calls it her ninja suit. She likes to joke around and make her grandchildren laugh.

The Grandchildren and Their Parents

She visits her grandchildren every Wednesday at five in the evening, she has two grandchildren and adores them. Her granddaughters name is Kyna, shes eight years old and is always exploring, the backyard.

Although she doesn't like insects, she doesn't like to hear loud noises. She has blue eyes and when she was just three years old.

She had a bad habit of putting everything in her mouth and, would cry for half the night. But her parents are always looking out for her.

Her other granddaughters name is Taniya and she is five years old and loves to sleep. She doesn't like mornings and prefers to stay up until nine o clock at night.

Her mother Taylor is a night owl and some nights she stays up all night. Then the next morning she's absolutely exhausted.

Taylor is a very responsible mother and when she puts her daughter in the car she makes sure that she is properly strapped in. Taylor does the speed limit and prefers not to speed. Even when she is driving on the highway she doesn't like to drive in the passing lane. She drives a new 2016 red dodge Caravan. Her van gets okay gas mileage, but at the end of the week she spends forty-five dollars to fill up the gas tank.

She takes good care of her van and even knows how to do an oil change, she refuses to pay for a mechanic to change her vans oil. Just last Tuesday she was almost in a serious accident.

She saw the car coming at her in the wrong lane and was able to swerve out of the way and barely missed getting hit.

The driver who was driving was just some young punk kid who thought that it was so cool to speed.

He was driving an old junker 1966 mustang
hardtop.

His car crashed into a telephone pole, and it didn't
seem to slow down his car. He crashed into the
front entrance of a grocery store. The whole front of
his car was bent in, and the front bumper fell off.

Black smoke came bellowing up out of the engine.
The driver hit his head on the steering wheel and
was knocked unconscious. Ten minutes after the
accident, the local Police Department showed up.

It turned out that the kid was just twenty-two years
old and one year prior had his license taken away
from him for driving drunk after leaving a college
party.

Taylor wants to have one more child, her husband
loves her dearly, and they go out to dinner together
twice a week.

They don't always eat very healthy. Taylor's
favorite food is pizza, she says if she could, she
would eat pizza every day, but her husband doesn't
like it when she eats so much junk food.

He is a dietician and eats well, and at times can be
very controlling. Taylor is engaged to him, and they
are very happy together.

Taylor has many girlfriends and Friday nights she
goes out to the local bar and has a few drinks, while
her husband watches over the children. Her
husband's name is Chow.

He's a short fellow and comes from a big family who used to live in China and now lives in the United States. He's thirty-four years old and is such a kind loving person.

He likes to give hugs. Although Taylor doesn't like it when Chow drives because he likes to speed, and is not a cautious driver like Taylor is.

Chow likes to keep in a routine, and hasn't gone on a vacation for many years and is planning on trying to go on a cruise in the next few months.

He wants to go on a cruise to the Caribbean, but Taylor would rather take a cruise to Alaska. Chow and Taylor very rarely get into arguments. Taylor and Chow like to drink wine late in the evening.

Although Taylor and Chow don't like to watch much television. Taylor likes to read romantic novels. But Chow likes to read hunting and fishing magazines.

One-night Chow was reading a motorcycle magazine, chow likes to ride his motorcycle. He has a triumph and got it from a respected Harley Davidson dealer.

He paid twenty-five thousand dollars, and Taylor didn't like that Chow had bought a motorcycle and warned him not to ride it, or he could be killed.

Chow is very cautious while he is riding his motorcycle. He does the speed limit, but speeds when he goes on the highway.

Chow has been riding his bike for going on five years now and doesn't regret riding on nice sunny days.

Each day he drives his bike to work and everyone at work knows when he pulls into the parking lot.

He replaced the regular tail pipes with custom pipes that made the bike much louder. He wears a black helmet with the sticker on it that says loud pipes save lives.

Although none of his coworkers, own a motorcycle but wish they did. One of his coworkers is jealous that he owns a motorcycle. Taylor doesn't like it when Chow comes home late on a Saturday night.

Bernice checks in with Chow and Taylor twice every week. Bernice likes to eat Chinese food, but prefers to make it herself.

Bernice learned to cook from her grandmother and mother. Her grandmother is half Irish and Italian.

Bernice lives in a sub division and is good friends with all of her neighbors, she likes to say hi to newspaper boy. Who comes to her house at seven o clock in the morning.

Bernice doesn't mind the newspaper boy coming to her house so early. Bernice likes to wake up at six o clock in the morning and get herself ready for the day.

Since Bernice is older she doesn't prefer to wear dresses. She has five dresses in her closet that she no longer wears.

About a week ago she had a yard sale and sold all of her dresses for twenty dollars. The women that bought her clothes was twenty-eight years old and was planning on having two more kids.

She was a nice women and she drove an old Honda van. She gave Bernice the money and right afterwards took off down the road.

Bernice's house is well kept, and she dusts the house every day. Her house has three bedrooms and two baths, and an attic. She has a finished basement where she keeps her old dining room table set.

Bernice still has her grandmothers fine China and keeps it in the basement. Bernice's neighbor who lives off to the left of her is an old woman who's in her late nineties and her husband is eighty. Bernice has long white blinds and a pretty blue certain that covers the top of the blinds.

Chapter 1: The Neighbors

One day Bernice was dusting the window sill and opened the blinds and looked out, and saw her neighbor Dale and Corrine were sitting out on their front porch.

Their eyes were focused on a little yellow bird that had landed in the bird bath. The bird seemed to be content in the bird bath and remained there for a few minutes.

Then flew away. Dale and Corrine looked away from the bird and were watching their young neighbor as he cut the grass. All of a sudden Dale sneezed so hard that his glasses fell off of his face, so Corrine came over and picked up his glasses and placed them back on his face.

Bernice kept on watching the elderly couple. Dale stood up and walked back into his house and Corrine followed along with him.

Dale had a slight limp and made him walk much slower. Bad backs run in his family, and he is slightly bent over but he doesn't let it stop him from walking.

He wears white slip on shoes, which his wife Corrine helps him to put them on. He won't let her tie his shoe laces, he still ties them with no difficulty.

Corrine tells him to pick up his feet while he walking, but he just ignores her. However, she is persistent and eventually he picks up his feet.

He says that he has trouble lifting up his feet, but she knows otherwise. One time he was walking out of the Drs. office and tripped over the small lip in the doorway.

He fell forward on his face, his glasses shattered and he could barely get himself up again, luckily one of the nurses saw what had happened and walked over by him and helped him get back up.

He had some minor scratches on his forehead and was complaining of his lower back hurting him.

The nurse took him back into the Drs office and fixed up his face. Corrine couldn't stop thanking the nurse for her help, Corrine was just thankful that the nurse was there.

Dale yelled out, I don't remember where I am, the nurse said my name is nurse Yeats. Don't worry Dale its going to be okay, you're in the Drs. Office.

"How did I get here?"

"Your wife drove you here."

"I am cold Yeats; can you turn up the temperature in here?"

"Yes," I can.

Corrine stood right next to the chair that her husband was sitting in. Dale looked over at Corrine and asked how long have I been here for? You have been here for ten minutes so far. Yeats leaned over behind Dales back and whispered into his wife's right ear.

"Do you know if your husband has dementia?"

"No," I don't know.

"Can I have him tested for it?"

"Yes," you can.

"Can the test be scheduled for today?"

"No," I'm sorry but I can't.

"Hey what are you two whispering about behind my back?"

"Were talking about what we are going to do for you on your up and coming. birthday celebration. You're my wife and I love you, but you have to stop keeping secrets from me. "

You don't have to worry about what we are talking about. But I'm concerned what you are talking about with the nurse.

"Have you ever heard the word Dementia?"

"No"

"What is it?"

"It's something that happens to you when you're an old man."

"Does everyone get it when they get old?"

"No," it all depends on the person.

"What are you looking at Yeats?"

I'm looking at you Dale, we'll stop looking at me, it's irritating me.

"Dale are you always this irritable?"

"No," I just don't like it when women stare into my eyes like they are looking for something.

"What could I be looking for in your eyes Dale?"

"I don't know, and I don't care."

"Were you shy as a young man Dale?"

"No," and some habits never change."

"Now how much longer do I have to sit here doing nothing?"

"Just until I feel that you are healthiest to leave here."

I didn't like my Dr. and I would like to get another Dr.

"Why didn't you like about Dr Dale?"

"He was a young man and didn't answer all of the questions that I had for him."

He acted like a young punk and came across to me that he was a know it all. I don't like know it all's, he wasn't very patient with me. He took his whatever it was a listened to my heart with it.

It's called a stethoscope Dale, thanks for telling me, you interrupted what I was saying. So can I continue my story now Yeats, Yes you may.

The Dr. pressed the stethoscope hard into my chest and back and really irritated me.

"Did you tell him that?"

"No," I just let him go.

He had bad breath and his teeth were all yellow, that's not really his fault. But he should brush his teeth and not let them get yellow.

Maybe he drinks a lot of coffee Dale, no stop making up excuses for the Dr. He knows that he needs to brush his teeth. Not everyone has good hygiene Dale.

I don't care what you say about hygiene. Would you stop being a grumpy old man, no I won't. I'm sick and tired of hearing you complain about the Dr. Just be happy that the Dr looked you over.

"Do you take mood pills?"

"No," I don't even know what a mood pill is and looks like.

I don't like to take pills, I would rather crush them up and just drink them down.

"What do you take your pills with?"

"I take them with my ensure and the Dr. makes me drink ensure. I don't even like the taste of ensure."

The Dr. says that I'm not eating enough. So, I have to sit at my dam kitchen table with my wife and she won't let me leave the table until I have drunk down one can of ensure.

"How many cans of ensure do you drink a day?"

"I forget, how about if I ask your wife, he drinks two cans of ensure."

Chapter 2: Housework

It's always such a battle to make him drink a whole can. He drinks half and tells me that he had enough, then I have to encourage him to finish it. I can't believe that you are telling all this to the nurse.

"Would you please be quiet?"

"No," I won't, and you should keep your mouth closed about our personal matters.

"Now you see how ugly he can get?"

"I can see that he's quick to anger."

"Do you read the newspaper?"

"I used to read the newspaper, but I lost interest in it."

I would read the newspaper from front to back and by the time I was done reading it, then I realized that I had forgotten half of what I had read and it makes me so frustrated.

Cleaning the House

Bernice then closed up the blinds, she heard something making a buzzing sound. She looked up at the ceiling fan and there was a stink bug flying around it. The light in the fan was turned on and this must have attracted the stink bug.

The stink bug kept on buzzing around and landed on Bernice's left shoulder and Bernice's couldn't stand the sight of the bug and with her right hand she flicked the bug off of her shoulder and it landed on the floor by her left foot.

She does everything in such a proper manner. She walked over to her coffee table and there was her dark blue tissue box, she carefully took out one tissue and walked back over where the stink bug was. The stink bug crawled under her tan reclining chair.

She kept on watching for the bug, but he didn't come out. So she got down on her hands and knees and looked under the chair.

Suddenly the stink bug came flying out from beneath the leather recliner. The bug scared her so Much that she backed away from the recliner so fast she that she bumped into her coffee table.

The Kleenex box fell onto the floor and so did a large pile of magazines. All the magazines were better homes and gardens magazines.

Bernice's hat fell off of her head and landed right by the fire place, she quickly crawled over for fear that her hat was going to burn up.

She took off her white gloves and set them on the left-hand corner of the coffee table. She didn't like

being on the floor anymore, so she leaned on the
coffee table and was able to get herself up.

Once she was up she heard the squealing sound of
her tea pot and said oh dear and went running into
the kitchen and turned off the burner on the stove.

The water was still boiling, she said oh dear again
and some boiling water splashed onto the floor, she
backed up and moved the rug that was in front of
the stove. She took the rug and put it in the living
by the coffee table.

She went back into the kitchen and looked in the
Cubert. And took out a large coffee mug and placed
it by the stove.

She forgot all about the stink bug that was crawling
around her living room. Oh what A slop I am, I
can't believe that I spilled water on the floor again.
Suddenly her doorbell rang off twice, the bell itself
wasn't very loud and she could barely hear it. She
opened the front door and it was her neighbor
Corrine.

    "What's the matter?"

    "It's my husband, he threw a can of ensure
    at me and it went all over the wall in our
    kitchen."

I can barely catch my breath so hold on a moment.
It's okay, take your time. So then I looked over at
my husband and he was drooling.

He had his face down on the kitchen table. I walked over to him and he didn't even move. He still had a pulse but it was barely there.

I called 911 and they dispatched an ambulance right away. So why are you telling me this Corrine, because you're a good friend of mine and are so understanding.

>"Where's your husband now?"

>"He's in the ER and I need to go see him now."

>"Would you mind watching over my house for the day?"

>"No," here's the key to my house, thank you.

I want you to go over to my house as soon as you can, I will, don't worry I'll keep your safe house.

>"Why don't you get a security system put in?"

>"No," I would rather come over here and ask you to watch my house.

Besides that, a new security system is very pricy, I refuse to spend thousands of dollars for a security system. You're never going to be able to convince me to buy a security system. I should get going now, alright I'll see you later then. Let me get the

door for you, no thanks I can get the door by
myself.

Corrine opened the door and never turned back. By
now Corrine, and Corrine never turned back to see
that Bernice was waving bye to her.

Bernice walked back into her house and sat down
on a chair in her kitchen. Suddenly she had urge for
an egg, she took out a pan and placed it on top on
the stove.

Then she walked over to the refrigerator and opened
it, she looked in and couldn't seem to find any eggs.

She dug through the crisper and all she could find
was broccoli and red beat eggs that she had made
two days ago.

She found some orange juice and opened the bottle
and smelled it. It had a foul odor and she made a
funny face.

She grabbed the bottle and threw it in the trash can.
She didn't make the lid tight enough and it spilled
all over the place in the trash can.

The trash can was now over loaded and it was time
for her to take out the trash. But before she even
touches the trash can she puts on sterile gloves and
puts a mask over her face. The mask looks like a
cat's face. She had bought this mask at a yard sale
two weeks ago.

When Bernice was a child she would refuse to go trickier or treating, because her parents wouldn't go with her and forced her to go with friends. Bernice keeps her gloves in her bedroom on her night stand. She keeps her extra gloves in her closet.

Bernice likes to wear sweaters and must own ten sweaters. She learned how to make her own sweaters a month ago. Bernice walked down the long hallway that leads back to her bedroom.

She walked over to her night stand and took out two sterile gloves from the box of gloves. She tried to put on one of the gloves and it ripped. Oh well that was just a cheap glove anyway and she threw the torn glove into the trash can.

She pulled out another glove and this glove didn't tear when she put it on. Now all she need now was her cat mask to take out the trash. She kneeled down by her bed and got the cat mask from beneath her bed.

She hadn't worn the mask for week, once she pulled the mask out from beneath her bed she placed it on top of her bed and saw that there was a dead stink bug in the mask.

Chapter 3: The Mop

She didn't dare to even touch the dead stink bug without gloves. She opened the one drawer of her dresser and took out a magnifying glass. Then she walked over to the mask and took a closer look at the dead stink bugs body.

Oh yuck what a horrible looking bug you are, the bugs legs were all sticking up. You know what bug you are messing with the wrong lady; I won't put up with you dying in my house.

I would like to know where you came from you disgusting bug. How dare you come into my house and stink it up.

You never asked me permission to come into my house. I've never saw a stink bug up close before.

Alright enough of me talking, Bernice picked up the dead stink bug and threw it into the trash can by her bed. Then she sniffed her hand and it was all stinky, oh yuck now my hand stinks. Oh my heavens.

I'm tired of touching these stinky stink bugs. She walked over to her bathroom sink and took off her gloves and looked at herself in the mirror. She threw away the gloves and immediately afterwards began to scrub her hands with a bar of ivory soap. Her wedding ring fell of her ring finger and almost went into the drain. Oh no my ring.

She quickly got all the soap off of her hands and then took a towel down from the rack that was off to the left of the sink.

She clenched her ring in her left hand so tightly that it made a mark on her hand. She thought to herself well that was a close call. She took her ring along with her as she walked back over to her bed.

She carefully placed her ring back on her ring finger and went on with her business. She picked up the mask and placed it over her face and put on another pair sterile gloves. Then she walked out of her bedroom and realized that she had forgot to turn the light off.

So she walked over by the light switch and switched it off. She thought to herself I am being very forgetful lately.

She remembered that she had forgot to wash her hair this morning. Then she left her bedroom and went back out to the kitchen. She forgot to grab the mop and was very upset with herself. She walked half way down the hallway and opened the door to her cleaning closet.

As she opened the door a cob web hit it in the forehead. Oh yuck what an awful place to have an old cob web. She brushed the cob web away from her face and went on looking for a mop. She could smell the faint smell of mold. Oh my goodness I can't believe that I have mold in my house.

She thought to herself oh I'll have to have the mold removed from my house again. Bernice went into a cleaning fit and took the mop and bucket out of the moldy closet.

She looked down at the bottom of the bucket and noticed that there were dead moths and stink bugs in the bottom of it.

She must have counted five dead stink bugs and three dead moths. Oh this closet really stinks and she took her left hand and pinched her nose shut.

Once she got the mop and bucket out of the closet she slammed the door to the closet with all the remaining strength that she had. She took the mop and bucket along with her as she went back into the kitchen and placed the bucket in the center of the kitchen, and she picked up the mop and began to clean the floor, with it.

She has had this mop for five years and it now its fall apart. As she was cleaning the hardwood floor, with the mop, a stink bug came flying into the room and buzzed around her head.

Get out of here you stinky stink bug. I'm just trying to get some work done here and you have to come in here and interrupt me. You stink bugs have no regard for my house and make my house stink.

She kept on cleaning up the floor and decided that after just ten minutes that she was done cleaning. Oh I'm so tired of cleaning this house. She brought the bucket over to the sink and placed the mop in the bucket. She peered out the kitchen window and saw her neighbor Mr. Miller, was out in his yard filling up the bird feeder. It was just eight o clock in the morning and Bernice was already so tired.

She kept on watching Mr. miller, she saw two squirrels running along on the telephone pole wires. One of the squirrels had an acorn in his mouth.

While the other squirrel was trying to take it from him. Bernice grew tired of watching the two squirrels and got back to cleaning up the kitchen, she could barely even lift the bucket up, but with her iron will was able to lift it up and placed it in the sink and used the sprayer at the sink to clean out the water. She put the bucket back down and then proceeded to place the mop back in the bucket.

She once again took the mop and bucket, back to the cleaning supply closet and quickly put the bucket and mop back in the closet.

She quickly closed the closet and went back into her living room and grabbed the rug and took it back into the kitchen.

She placed it back down in front of the stove. The top of her stove was absolutely filthy and had not been cleaned in a week. Bernice doesn't like to clean the top of the stove.

She still had the mask on her face and so now she decided to empty the trash can and take out the trash.

She took the trash out and threw the big black bag
of trash in her garage. The mask was making her
face all sweaty and she was tired of it, so she took it
off and it fell down by her feet.

The garage was kind of dark and she couldn't see
very well, so she reached around looking for the
light switch.

She found the light switch and she was getting more
stressed out. She flicked on the light switch and the
light didn't come on. She thought to herself well
that's odd and now I have to replace the light bulb.

She was feeling like going on the hunt for the stink
bug again. She walked into her living room and the
stink bug was now in the middle of the living room.

I got you now and there will be no escape for you
this time you silly little stink bug. She leaned on the
recliner and bent over and forgot that she didn't
have a Kleenex in her left hand.

So she took out a Kleenex and started over again
looking for the stink bug. Lucky for her the stink
bug stayed in one place.

Now she reached down again and grabbed the stink
bug and crushed it in Kleenex. Now I got you.
Bernice was barely able to get up but used the
recliner to help her get back up again.

Once she stood back up she headed to the trash can
in the kitchen, and threw the Kleenex in it. She

thought to herself oh Lordy I'm getting tired. Then she thought on I'm so glade that I had off today.

She was feeling tired so she sat down in her tan recliner, and said out loud oh it feels so good to finally sit down again.

She put her head back and reclined back. She thought to herself, I have so much to do yet. All of a sudden she heard someone yelling.

It sounded like Mr. Miller. Bernice figured that he must have hurt himself while mowing the lawn.

Chapter 4: Train ride

Mr. miller likes to mow his lawn at eight fifty-five in the morning. Bernice can't understand why he likes to mow his lawn so early in the morning. Bernice sat in her chair for ten minutes and then got up.

She said out loud oh my poor back is aching again, she carefully got herself back up and decided that it was time for her to go over and check on her neighbor's house.

She made sure that all the burners on the stove were turned off. Then she opened her front door and walked out. She remembered that she put Corrine's key in her left pocket. She reached down into her pocket and retrieved the key, the key was made out of bronze and was dull. She carefully walked over to the front door of her neighbor's house and put the key in the lock and turned the dooknob and the door opened right up.

She slowly strolled into the house. She walked into the living and saw that Corrine had left the television on and the volume was turned all the way up, but she could find the tv remote.

She looked around the coffee table and then searched the couch. It was a large black leather couch. Meanwhile her great uncle Arnie got on the train headed to Nova Scotia. He placed his briefcase on the top rack and sat near the window side.

He pulled out his napkin and wiped his nose as he had a slight cold. Arnie then looked around the cabin and sighed softly. He took out another napkin from his pocket, stood up and began to clean the train.

While he's doing so, another passenger stops outside Arnie's cabin and looks at him. Arnie is busy cleaning. He only looks back at the new passenger when he turns around to clean the door.

Arnie stops and looks at the passenger with a surprised expression. The new passenger has a dead-pan expression on his face.

"Can I come in?"

"Is this your cabin?" Arnie asked.

"Yes."

"Then come in."

"But you're cleaning."

"Do you want to help me clean?"

"If you want to."

"But I hate cleaning," The passenger said, "I don't even clean my own room."

"Then you would have to wait."

"But I don't want to wait. I want to sit."

"But I didn't finish cleaning."

"Then clean it later."

"But look at how dirty the cabin is," Arnie said.

"It's not that dirty," The passenger said.

"It is," Arnie said and pointed around the cabin,

"Look at the seats, they are so dirty, the windows, they're so foggy, and even the floor! It's like some beast just threw up in here."

The passenger poked his head inside the cain and looked around. After examining the cabin, he looks back at Arnie.

"Are you sure your eyes aren't dirty?" The
passenger asked.

"What?"

"Are you making fun of me?"

"That's because I don't see anything dirty,
Sir."

"So then your eyes must be dirty because
you can't see any dirt!"

The passenger rolled his eyes

"Can you please let me in and take my seat?

I'm already tired enough after fighting from
my wife!"

"Oh, I'm so sorry that you fought with your
wife, kind sir,"

Arnie said apologetically, "Please, do come
in and take a seat. You have been through a
battle, I see!"

Arnie stepped aside and the passenger finally
entered the cabin, placed his bag on the upper rack
and sat down. Arnie cleaned his seat, put the napkin
in a plastic bag and put the bag inside his briefcase.

However, just as Arnie was about to sit, the
passenger sneezed and his sneeze spread on Arnie's
seat.

"Sorry about that," The passenger sniffed.

"Arnie sighed annoyedly and tried to find a
napkin in his pocket, but he didn't have
any."

"It's okay, my sneeze isn't dirty at all!" The
passenger grinned. Arnie looked around to try and
find a clean spot to sit, but he didn't find any.
Eventually, he sat on his seat while grimacing.

"I'm Ronnie," The passenger said,

"What's your name?"

Mr. Too Clean For You?"

Ronnie laughed out loud while slapping his
thighs.

"No, I hate that name.

"Who even has that kind of name?" Arnie
said,

"My name's Arnie Roberts and I'm from
England."

"Oh, quite the sophisticated place you're from,"
Ronnie said in a fake British accent,

"What did you eat for breakfast today?
English?"

Arnie pinched his temples as he couldn't take
anymore of Ronnie's absurdity.

"Come on, that was a funny joke!"

Ronnie whined, "You gotta be loose sometimes, you know."

"I don't like to be loose," Arnie said,

"What do you mean by loose?"

"Do you think I'm a pant to be loose or tight?"

Ronnie chuckled at that, "See, that was a good joke and that's called being loose!"

"I don't get you. You're weird."

"People do call me weird."

"Yes, and they aren't wrong."

"I'll take that as a compliment, actually," Ronnie said proudly.

Arnie didn't respond back. In fact, he looked out the window and wished how soon he could reach his destination.

"So where you off to?" Ronnie asked.

"I'm not comfortable sharing such details with you."

Ronnie gasped, "I'm hurt by that. You have a sharp tongue."

"I do get that a lot."

"Then why didn't you blunt it?"

Chapter 5: The Talk

Ronnie laughed out loud. Arnie shook his head in disbelief.

"Could you please choose your words correctly?"

"What's wrong with my words?"

It's not like I'm saying some bad language or anything. English is meant to be funny and used as one wishes, don't you think?"

"I do not think so, no."

"Then you're crazy because one shouldn't be so strict with stuff."

"Who said I'm strict?"

"Your words did!" Ronnie smirked as he thought he had made quite the genius comment.

Arnie then got up from his seat and peeked outside the cabin.

"Hey, what are you doing?" Ronnie asked.

Arnie looked back at Ronnie, "I'm trying to find the conductor."

"The conductor?" Ronnie frowned,

"Why?"

"Because I want to change my cabin."

"Why do you want to change your cabin?"

"Because you're annoying me."

"But I didn't do anything, did I?"

"No, but I'm still annoyed by you."

Ronnie sighed, "Okay, I'll be the bigger guy here and apologize first. I'm sorry."

"No, I won't let you be the bigger guy. I'll be the bigger guy and I already forgave you!"

Arnie grunted as he sat back down on his seat. Ronnie shrugged and pulled out a sandwich from his bag.

"Do you want some?" He asked Arnie.

"No, thank you."

"Are you sure? This sandwich is delicious. My wife made it for me."

"Before you left?"

"Yes."

Arnie frowned softly, "No, I mean, does she know that you're getting away from her?"

"Oh yes, she was the one to kick me out of the house after making me the sandwich."

Arnie's eyes grew wide, "I thought it was the opposite!"

"Well, you thought wrong buddy."

Ronnie opened the sandwich box and began eating it.

"What happened with you and your wife? If you don't mind me asking," Arnie asked.

"Of course I mind!" Ronnie said annoyedly this time"

"Why do you want to know what goes on between me and my wife, huh?"

"Mind your own business!"

Arnie flinched ever so slightly and his cheeks turned red in embarrassment. "I'm…I'm sorry…" He mumbled and glanced at Ronnie who was seriously eating his sandwich.

Arnie pursed his lips and decided not to talk about anything anymore. Before Arnie knew it, he had fallen asleep.

When he woke up, he noticed that Ronnie wasn't in his seat. Arnie rubbed his eyes and he let out a sigh of relief as he thought that Ronnie had finally got off his stop, but poor Arnie was wrong.

Ronnie came inside the cabin while wiping his wet hands on his pants. He sat in his seat and looked at Arnie with a big smile on his face.

"You sleep well?" Ronnie asked.

"Yes…Thank you." Arnie sat up straighter and adjusted his coat.

"How about you? Didn't you sleep?"

"Naw, I hate sleeping in trains."

"Why?"

"Because you never know who can steal
your stuff.

Arnie frowned softly, "I'm sure no one will steal
anything from the passengers, Ronnie. This is a safe
train and only good and mannered people come to
this coach."

"Huh, are you sure about that Arnie?"

"Why, yes, of course."

"You better change your perspectives then
because it's not right to trust just anyone."

Arnie simply rolled his eyes and looked out the
window again. Everything outside was a blur but
pretty too.

Arnie wondered how his life would have been if he
was a Superman or some kind of a flying superhero.
Perhaps he wouldn't have had to meet people like
Ronnie because he wouldn't have the need to take a
train.

"So, Arnie, tell me about yourself," Ronnie
suddenly asked.

"Sorry, but I'm not comfortable doing so."

Ronnie sighed, "Then what are you
comfortable in doing so?'

"Not talking to you." Arnie smiled.

Ronnie laughed, "That was a good one!"

"I'm not joking."

"Oh, I know you are, you don't have to
explain the joke, Arnie, you know that,
right?"

Arnie couldn't help it anymore. He actually wanted
to scream out loud and maybe even bang his head to
the wall.

He obviously couldn't do any of that sort. He had to
gulp his anger and make sure that he doesn't hurt
his passenger.

"So, tell me."

Arnie figured out that Ronnie isn't going to stop, so
he eventually told him a little about himself. Arnie
was thirty-three, not married, working as an IT
Engineer at North Valley and struggling to buy a
house and a car. Ronnie didn't seem interested in
Arnie's details though. Arnie could make that out
just from his expression.

"Tell me about yourself now," Arnie said
once he was done talking about himself.

Ronnie blew raspberries, "No way I'm
going to share my life story with a complete
stranger like you!"

"But I told you, didn't I?"

"That's your fault," Ronnie said, shrugging,
"I told you not to trust anyone."

Chapter 6: Discomfort

Arnie groaned and got up at once. He glared down at Ronnie before storming out of the cabin.

He went to the bathroom, peed and while washing his hands, stared at himself in the mirror.

"Why do I get people like that?" He wondered aloud, "If he continues to irritate me, I might just push him out of the train–

No, you need to have calm thoughts…No violent thoughts…"

Arnie breathed in and out as a form of meditation. Once he was done breathing, he went back to his cabin, only to find his acquaintance fast asleep. Ronnie was snoring loudly. His head kept falling to the side because of the train's movement and he was drolling.

Arnie frowned and his nostrils flared as he saw the way Ronnie slept. Arnie didn't like it. He liked clean sleeping and Ronnie wasn't sleeping clean or right!

Arnie tried to ignore Ronnie once, twice, and even thrice but at the forth time, he just couldn't take it anymore.

Arnie pulled out his clean handkerchief, got up, walked over to Ronnie and began cleaning his drool. After all, Arnie hated anything dirty and in his eyes, drool was dirty.

A dirt that came out of someone's mouth and made their faces smell like a throw-up. As Arnie was cleaning, Ronie jolted awake by his touch and looked at Arnie as though he was some kind of a gang member.

"What are you doing?!" Ronnie pushed Arnie behind and placed his arms over his chest in a criss-cross fashion.

Just like how a woman would do if she was ever touched by a man–by mistake or purposefully.

"I was just "

"Get away from me!" Ronnie pushed Arnie behind and got up.

Arnie got pushed back to his seat and he looked up at his passenger with wide and confused eyes.

"I'm going to call the cops and tell them that you were trying to sexually abuse me!"

"Wait, no, you got it wrong"

"No, I know exactly what you were trying to do, Arnie!"

Ronnie shook his head, "I should
have known the moment I saw you
clean the cabin like a distressed
female…"

"Female?"

"What are you even saying?"

"I was just trying to clean the drool off of
your face."

"So what if I drool?" Ronnie said
defensively, "It's my drool, it's my wish."

"No, I didn't mean it like–"

Ronnie placed both his hands on his hips,
"Oh, I know exactly what you meant,
mister," He narrowed his eyes at Arnie.

"Okay, I'm sorry…" Arnie said softly,
"Could you please not make a scene right
now."

Arnie didn't want the entire train to think that he
was some kind of a weirdo or a pervert or
something. He just wanted to reach his destination
safe and soundly.

"Fine, but when we're getting down, you're
buying me food."

"Wait, why should I–"

"Hello?!" Ronnie suddenly started yelling,

"Is anyone there"

"Okay! Okay!" Arnie said quickly to shut Ronnie up, "I'll not only feed you dinner but dessert too, so please shut up."

Ronnie simply sat back down and crossed his leg on top of one another. Arnie pinched his temples again and tried not to think too.

He knew he was getting played, but Ronnie was smart. He didn't expect something like this would happen!

Fifteen minutes later, the train eventually came to a stop. Arnie couldn't have been happier to get down from the train. He quickly grabbed his suitcase and was about to dash when

"Hey, Arnie, aren't you forgetting something?"

Arnie stopped and looked back at Ronnie, "What?"

Ronnie swayed his hands over his own self, "Me! Did you forget our deal already?"

Arnie wished Ronnia had forgotten about their weird incident but Ronnie didn't.

"Okay, let's go"

Arnie and Ronnie got out of the train.

"I'm so excited!" Ronnie squealed in excitement. Arnie could only run his hands through his hair.

As Arnie was walking, Ronnie followed him. Arnie was in the lead of course. He had thought once or twice about simply running away from Ronnie or tricking him.

Then running away, but no matter what he planned, he didn't have the confidence to execute it. In the end, both of them entered a restaurant and ordered food and dessert of their liking.

"Thank you so much, Arnie!" Ronnie said enthusiastically, "I can't believe you fell for my trick!"

Arnie frowned, "What trick?"

"Oh nothing, I opened my big mouth again, oops," Ronnie laughed out loud.

Arnie wasn't sure what to say or how to react, but he kept his composure as best he could. Once the food and desserts arrived, Arnie and Ronnie both ate in silence.

They enjoyed their meals and even though Arnie was annoyed at Ronnie for irritating him, he had forgotten all aout it because of the delicious food they had. Arnie paid for the meal and the two came out with a full-stomach.

"Thank you again, I hope to meet you soon again sometime."

"No, please don't…" Arnie thought to himself but he just smiled at Ronnie and nodded.

"Do you want to share numbers?"

"Think fast, don't give him your number…" But Arnie's thoughts never really were in sync with his mouth, "Sure. It's xxx-xxx-xxxx."

Ronnie saved the number with a wide smile and nodded, "Thank you, I'll message you soon!"

Arnie nodded, "Yes, you should go now. I'm going this way."

"You got it, friend!" Ronnie punched Arnie's shoulders, laughed, waved at Arnie and walked away.

Chapter 7: Frustration

As Ronnie was walking away, Arnie let out a sigh of relief. He then pulled out his phone, opened his camera, turned on the selfie mode and looked at himself.

"Why do you always have to share your details with strangers?" Arnie asked himself.

He then turned off his phone, took out his sim card and after crushing it, threw it in a dustbin before walking home.

"How he can't call me, can he?" Arnie smirked.

It took him a while to get home because he had stopped at a bakery to get himself a nice, big loaf of fresh bread for tomorrow morning's breakfast and then went to the florist to bring a bouquet of fresh flowers for his girlfriend, Lillian.

Arnie wanted to go home, but he didn't. He decided to surprise Lillian because he loved her and he just wanted to surprise her for fun.

Besides, it had been a while since he had done anything romantic for her, so this was a great way to spark their romance.

Arnie stopped outside Lillian's door and rang the doorbell. A few minutes later, Lillian opened the door but she was breathing heavily, wearing her pink robe and her hair was disheveled.

"A-Arnie?" She said, stuttering as she looked at him from head to toe, unable to believe that Arnie was even thee in front of her eyes.

"Yes, Lillian, it's me, Arnie, your boyfriend.

"Did you forget me already?"

Arnie asked, "Why are you even breathing hard?"

"Is it your asthma?"

"Arnie asked worriedly as he gently pushed Lillian aside and stepped inside her house."

"I know where your inhaler is. It's in the bedroom, right"

"No, don't go in there"

But it was already too late. Arnie, with his long strides, had already reached the bedroom door. He opened it and when he looked inside, his heart was in his mouth—well, his fist was in his mouth because he was biting himself from screaming. Ronnie was on Lillian's bed. Butt naked.

He looked at Arnie and gave a huge smile, "Hey friend!"

"Did you miss me already that you came running back to me?"

Arnie slowly looked to his side and saw Lillian smiling hesitantly while running a hand through her blonde hair.

Arnie knew what his next move would be, he must have been dumb once, but not now he knew just what to do. Arnie went back home and slept, hoping he would wake up only to find that all of this was just a nightmare. Now back with Bernice and her endless cleaning routine.

Sadly, the truth is, that life is harsh and you don't always get the lemons, or the sugar and the water, to make your lemonade.

There were some rips in the arms of the one recliner that was nestled in the left hand corner of the room. To the right of the black leather recliner was a bookshelf.

There were so many books on the shelf that there was no room for no other books. The shelf didn't look to be in good condition, there was a large crack going down the left side of the shelf. The books had a thick layer of dust and cob webs on them.

The television was still blaring and was really getting on her nerves. The news was on and the lady reporting the news had a raspy voice.

This only made her search even harder for the television remote. She walked back over to the black leather couch and began to search it again.

She put her hands down in between the fabric of the couch and she still couldn't find anything. In frustration she got down on her hands and knees and looked beneath the couch. She saw the controller but couldn't reach it, this made her frustrated so she looked around the room for a yard stick. But there was no yard stick, to be found in the living room. She walked out of the living room and into the kitchen. She opened the closet that was near the kitchen and hundreds of moths came flying out and she couldn't believe how many moths there were in the closet.

She quickly closed the closet door and stood directly in front of it. She left out a sigh and then got back to it.

She found an old mop in the back corner of the kitchen, the mop was filthy and the handle to it was bent.

But she didn't care about the shape it was in and took it back over to the living room couch. She got down on her hands and knees again and once again reached for the television remote. She used the broom handle and was able to finally reach the remote. She was able to get the remote and took her time getting back up.

The broom fell onto the ground and the handle fell off. She thought to herself oh well, I will have to fix that now. She was shaking her head in disgust and had her arms crossed.

She let out a moan and bent over and picked up the old broken broom. She walked over to the corner of the kitchen and placed the mop back where she had found it.

Then she walked over to the couch and picked up the remote and pointed it directly at the television.

But the television didn't go off. She threw her arms up in protest and sat down on the couch. The couch was so very comfortable, and was so easy for to her get comfortable on.

The television set was still blaring and was beginning to give her an awful headache. She thought to herself I wonder where she keeps her batteries. She thought on well maybe she stores the batteries in a battery drawer in the kitchen.

Then another thought came to her mind she thought now I'm going to have to search for the batteries.

She rubbed her left eye and let out another sigh, and said out loud oh bloody hell, I'm getting tired of house sitting and I haven't even got a minute to sit down to rest my old bones.

She heard a loud slam and this caused her to look around and her eyes got as big as saucers. She thought I hope it's not a cat, an all-white cat came

strolling into the living room and looked at her and
let out a meow.

"What are you looking at you dirty old
house cat?"

"I'm sure that you just came out so that I
could feed you."

Hey cat I'm not your mother and I don't know
where your food is. I don't feel like running all
around this big house and looking for your cat
Chow. You're just going to have to wait until your
mom gets back. You have pretty green eyes though,
but I still don't think you're in the least bit cute.

Please don't come any closer, you are a creepy cat,
I've never saw a cat stare as much as you do.

Chapter 8: Mr. Mittens

I'm allergic to cats, and so I can't pet you. I'm
surprised that Corrine didn't tell me that she had a
cat.

I guess I should have asked her about it. All of a sudden the front door swung open, and it was Corrine.

"Why are you back so soon? I forgot something"

"I have to ask you something, okay what is it?"

"Where is your battery drawer?"

"It's in the top drawer to the left side of the stove."

"Why do you store your batteries so close to the stove?"

I don't know, and if you don't like it then move them. You never mentioned to me that you had a cat, oh well now you know, but I am allergic to cats.

Alright well then just stay away from my cat then. That is hard to do because his long white hairs are all over everything.

All of a sudden Bernice's nose began to itch and she sneezed. God bless you Bernice, thanks Corrine, yeah no problem. Oh and one more thing, I don't have time for this,

Would you like a spot of tea?"

"I would but not now, I need to get back on the road."

"What did you forget?"

"That's none of your business, oh I see how it is. Listen I got to go now, just calm down and you don't need to know everything about a stranger's business."

You better not be snooping around my bedroom and this is my first and final warning. If I catch you going through my stuff in my bedroom I'll knock you for a real loop.

I don't like to be threatened by anyone, okay I threatened you and you can just get over it. Now you are just holding me up, I don't like it, let me go, you know that you are free to go. I think I know that.

"How's your husband doing?"

"He's doing just fine."

"Where is he today?"

"I don't know, he has off today and he told me that he was going to visit some old friends today."

"What's his name?"

"You forgot his name already?"

"Yes," I did, now what's his name?

"His name is Benson"

You have met him plenty of times before, yeah but I
forgot what he even looks like. He's a good looking
fellow; he's my hubby, I get along with him better
than I do with you Corrine. I heard about
enough, now I'm leaving. Good luck Corrine. I'll be
back in two days.

> "Aren't you going to tell me where the cats
> food is?"

> I would but you're allergic to cats so how
> would you feed my cat.

> "What's your cats name?"

> "It's a he and his name is Mr. Mittens."

> "Does he come when you call him?"

> "No," not always, just when he wants to
> come to me.

> "So you let your cat do whatever he wants?"

> "Yes," I do and don't do anything to my cat
> or I swear.

Oh my don't swear at me. But Mr. mittens will only
eat out his special bowl. Oh really so I can't use a
regular bowl from the sink.

No you can't, I'm only going to show you once
where his special bowl is. You better not lose his
special bowl or you'll be forced to buy him another
bowl.

51

I don't want you to feed him if it's after twelve o clock in the afternoon, why is that? If he eats after twelve o clock he gets indigestion and becomes so irritated with me.

"Does he use the toilet?"

"Yes," I trained him to use the toilet.

This cat can do a lot, yeah I love this cat, and don't let him go outside. If he gets outside you won't be able to catch him.

"How do you know that?"

"I don't have time to tell you the story. Bye now. Corrine walked out and slammed the front door behind her."

Bernice quickly walked into the kitchen and immediately began looking for the battery drawer. She looked in the drawer that Corrine had mentioned to look in.

The battery drawer was full to capacity with all kinds of batteries. There were double A's and Triple A's. there were even a few large D batteries.

The bottom of the drawer was full of think dust. The dust got between her fingers and she couldn't stand it.

She went over to the sink and began to wash her hands, oh yuck why must everything in this house be so dusty.

She didn't dare think about opening the closet door near the kitchen. So she went back over to the battery drawer and began to take out every battery that was in the drawer and place them down on the floor. There must have been sixty batteries, they were all different sized batteries. One of the batteries was all corroded, oh yuck these batteries stinks and is all corroded.

She took the corroded battery and threw it into the trash can. She went through the rest of the batteries, and found one other corroded battery and threw it out.

She bent over and began to pick up the batteries one at a time. She could feel that she was straining her back and was thinking about taking a short break. She looked over to her left and saw Mr. Mittens.

Oh no Mr. Mittens you can't come near me, I'm allergic to you. She let out a big sneeze that was so loud that it made Mr. Mittens run in the opposite direction.

It's okay Mr. Mittens it was just a sneeze. You can come back here if you would like. Mr. Mitten kept far away from Bernice, for the rest of the day.

She happened to look out the kitchen window and saw an all-black truck that had pulled up at the next door neighbor's house.

She kept her eyes peeled on the black truck. Suddenly the door opened and a tall bald man came out of the truck, he was wearing an all-black blazer and had on black pants. He had a cigarette hanging out of his mouth. He took out his lighter and lit up his cigarette and had a serious look on his face. His face was clean shaven and he had a scar on his nose.

He had green eyes and it seemed like he was nervous, he kept on watching behind his back, and looking off to his left. Then the next door neighbor opened her front door and allowed the man in.

Chapter 9: Bonding

Bernice was so surprised, that the women let the strange man into her house. Bernice wanted to see what the strange man was doing at the neighbor's house.

So she thought to herself how, am I going to get a better view at the neighbor's house. She looked back out the window and saw that the sky was beginning to cloud up. She heard some thunder in the distance.

She looked around for an umbrella, but couldn't find one. She walked over by the doorway and began looking for an umbrella. There was basket just a few feet away from the front door.

There was an extra set of keys and someday old peppermints. Bernice thought about throwing away the old peppermints but let it slip her mind and continued on looking for the umbrella.

Then she thought to look next to the book shelf in the living room. In the middle shelf was an old red umbrella.

The umbrella must have been sitting there for years, she bent down and picked up the umbrella. She looked it over good and then decided to open it.

When she pressed in the button the umbrella opened up and when it did, six dead stink bugs came falling out of the umbrella and went onto the floor.

She couldn't believe that there were stink bugs in the umbrella. She left the stink bugs lay on the floor and walked towards the front door.

She opened the door while she held onto the umbrella. She walked out the door and looked towards the neighbor's house, the neighbor's house had large tall green hedges growing along the right side of her house.

She looked closer at the hedges and saw that there was a little petite birds nest in the center of the hedges. A red robin was flying around the bird bath. Bernice was so interested in snooping on the neighbor that she did all she could to be able to look

in the neighbor's house. All of a sudden a drop of
water came down on her forehead.

It was beginning to rain, she had the umbrella right
over her head after feeling the first drop of rain.
There was a slight mist coming down along with the
rain.

She happened to look over at her house and saw that
her husband was pulling into the driveway. He got
out of the car and walked towards the front door and
he happened to look over and he saw Bernice.

> "What are you doing over at the neighbor's
> house?"

> "I'm supposed to watch over the neighbor's
> house."

It's starting to rain dear, maybe you should go
inside. I can't stand it seeing you staying out here in
the rain, oh dear I'm fine. Alright suit yourself then.
Talk to you later, bye now dear. Bernice hide
behind the tall green hedge and there was a window
a few feet away from the window. So she hid
behind the hedges and looked through the window.

She saw that the mystery man was sitting on the
couch with the neighbor. They were watching
television. she was glad to see that the man wasn't
hurting her.

Suddenly she saw that the man was peering out the
window and she quickly hid herself. Luckily the

man never seen her. She tip toed across the pavement towards the front of the house.

The pavement was all uneven and there was one puddle of black dirty water forming in the driveway. She walked over by the mail box and saw that the neighbors mail box was full of mail.

She took a moment an opened the big black mail box and letters and bills fell out, oh dear what have I done.

Oh the horrible bloody rain, she bent down and tried to pick up all the letters and bills. But it was too late, the letters and bills were all water logged and it was a real mess.

She bent down again and this time was able to pick up the rest of the letters. She took the wet and soggy letters and bills and placed them in the mailbox next to one that was open.

Oh dear I can't believe what I have done. She walked as quick as she could back over to her house.

She looked back and it was the mail man, he pulled up right next to the curb and seemed to be angry. She walked over to him.

"How are you doing?"

"I'm having a bad day, I don't like the rain. You know it's been a long time since I have seen you."

"Where have you been?"

"I have been at home, I just don't come out that often."

"How comes you are standing out in the rain?"

"I was just taking a walk around the neighborhood and it began to rain."

"How are your neighbors doing?"

"They're just fine and I'm getting tired."

"It's ten fifteen and you don't usually come around until three thirty."

"What's going on?"

I was late to work yesterday and the post master general made me come out early today. Okay I still find that to be odd, I have your mail for you, let me hand it to you.

He leaned over and picked up her mail from the passenger seat. Thank you so much for my mail. She looked through her mail and found a letter that was from her great aunt. I better get back on the road, but it's been good talking to you. Just remember to behave yourself.

"Why would you tell me to be behave?"

"You know me better than that."

I was just joking with you, try not to be so serious and learn to laugh, I do laugh a lot though, alright talk to you later, bye Hubert.

Hubert slowly drove down the road and went around the roundabout. It continued to rain but it didn't seem to bother her.

A red double decker tour bus drove past her, and some water splashed and hit her in the face and caused her make up to run all over her face. Oh dear how could that bus driver be so cruel.

She stormed off towards her front door, she happened to look in at the back seat and saw that there were some groceries in the back. Oh my goodness my husband is so forgetful.

She walked up the steps and opened her front door. She stepped inside and happened to look off to her left, and saw that her husband was sitting there watching television.

> "Hey dear, yes, how comes you are always watching the Telly?"

> "I got bored and decided to watch the Telly for a while."

> "What did you get done today?"

> "I just met with my friends and played a game of golf. Then I decided to come back here and relax. Before you get too

comfortable I want you to check on my
flowers."

They need to be watered, it's raining so they
don't need to be watered. What a perfect
excuse dear, you're lucky this time. You're
so demanding.

> "Would you please just sit here with
> me and relax"

"No," that's okay, I always have to be on the
move or my feet may fall asleep.

Oh come on sit down with me, you know that you
forgot some groceries in the car dear. I didn't
realize that I did that.

> "Are you going to get up and go get them
> for me?"

> "Yes," I will but not right now.

> "What's in the groceries bags dear?"

I bought some ring baloney and your favorite kind
of cheese.

> "I bought you some green tea bags and a
> blueberry cheese pie."

> "Can I get you a spot of tea dear?"

> "No," thanks I'm good thanks.

> "Aren't you going to get off of the couch?"

"No," not yet.

"What would get you moving?"

I don't know, I need to rest my aching knees. You never mentioned to me that you had knee pain, you need to learn to speak up dear. Don't worry about me, I'll be fine.

"What are you watching good?"

"I was just watching the news."

"Is there anything good on the news?"

"No," just the usual talk and none sense.

Hey look, the news women just said that the local mail man was in a fatal accident with a double decker bus. Oh my goodness, I just talked to him twenty minutes ago, that's so sad dear.

"Would you like a hug?"

"No," I don't need a hug

"Then why is your make up running all down your cheeks?"

"Because my face got splashed by water as a bus drove past me."

"Okay I understand"

"What did you get all over your shirt?"

"I was drinking some soda and some went on my shirt."

It's no big deal, yes, it's now let me have your shirt. Must I give you my shirt this moment, yes you do dear. I was in a good mood and now I'm not, please stop bothering me. No I won't stop bothering you, okay here's my shirt and let me go now.

"What are you looking at?"

"I'm looking at your hairy chest and it's really disgusting."

"I can't stand it; why must you keep on judging my looks?"

"I just know how I like to see you and I don't like to see a hairy chest."

You must wax your chest hair or I'll do it for you. No, dear I'm not going to wax my chest.

"Do you know how much that would hurt me?"

"Yes," I do and you will get over it.

Don't worry dear I'll hold your hand as my neighbor helps me to do the waxing.

"Why are you shaking dear?"

"I'm going to keep one open tonight, and I don't trust you. Oh you can trust me."

That's what you say now, but I know that you are going to wait until I fall into a deep sleep and then start the waxing process. No I wouldn't do that to you.

Although I have thought about some crazy schemes, the phone began to ring. Hurry up you know you don't have much time to get to the phone. She ran into the kitchen and got to the phone just in time.

"Hello who is this?"

"This is the post man general"

"Why are you calling me?"

I wanted to let you know that the mail man had just been in a fatal accident and now another mail man will be sent out, I'm sorry if you got your mail late today.

"No," I got my mail on time today.

"What's the new mail man's name?"

"Keck."

I've never heard of that name before; he must be special.

"Yes," he's special

"How old is he?"

I've never asked him that and its kind of odd for you to ask. I'm just a snoop, who likes to snoop in others people's business.

Chapter 10: The Officer

That's a bad habit, and you may get yourself in deep trouble being that way. No I know how to keep myself out of trouble. I would like to extend the conversation with you, but I have to go. It's alright.

"What are you really doing today?"

"It's my job to call everyone in your area and tell them about the mail man."

"How many more people do you have to call today?"

"I have to call hundred people and if I don't I'll get fired, do you have any more questions for me?"

"No," now I must go, okay bye now.

Bernice hung up the phone very carefully. Hey dear, what now. I got another letter from my great aunt.

"What does she want?"

"I don't know yet; I didn't find the time to open it."

"Would you like me to open it?"

"No," I know what happens when I let you have a letter, you always seem to lose it.

"I must read this letter to find out where she is traveling this time."

"Why must you know about every little thing that goes on?"

"That's just how I am, get used to it or get out."

"Did you really mean that?"

"Of course not dear, you must call me dear a hundred times per day. It's getting on my nerves."

"Then what do you want me to call you?"

"Don't just sit there shaking your head at me honey."

Yeah that's it, call me honey instead of dear, buts going to take some getting used to. What is that grimace for on your face dear?

You forget to call me honey instead of dear. I'm just not in a good mood and I thought about something funny.

"What's so funny?"

"You are," I wish it was quiet in here, but when your here it's never quiet. Oh you should bite your lip for saying that to me honey. No I won't take it back, you know that your loud and annoying.

Speak for yourself dear, when soccer is on you yell out at the Telly and you invite your cave men friends over. They just have long hair that goes down to their hips. Now that's where I draw the line.

I'm not going to allow you to talk about my friends like that. Your one friend looks like Paul McCartney. No he doesn't, he wasn't even related to him.

"Do you think before you speak?"

"Yes," I do, I don't believe that.

Now your nostrils are flaring again dear, I must have really upset you this time. We have been talking for almost an hour now and you still didn't find the time to go out to the car to get the groceries.

> "Isn't there something you should be doing?"

> "You wish, but I don't. Oh you poor man, I'm a good wife and you should be happy I'm always around."

> "Didn't you say that you had to check on your neighbor's house every so often?"

> "Yes," that's true, maybe I should get back over there, I sure wish you would. I see how you are now honey.

I'm fine here, now get a move on. Bernice gave her husband a dirty look and continued on with getting out the door. She opened the front door and the air felt thick, a light mist was coming down. The road was empty; no vehicles drove past her house. But she spied a police car patrolling along the streets.

The officer's car crept along at a slow pace. He seemed to be busy looking for someone or something. She went on with her business and went to walk over to her neighbor's house, all of a sudden the cop stopped and pulled over to the curb.

> "Excuse me Ma'am what is it you're doing on this ugly weather day?"

> "I was going over to my neighbor's house to make my neighbor a spot of tea."

"Oh how nice of you, but your neighbor's car isn't parked in her driveway."

"So what's going on?"

"Nothing really, her car is in the garage getting some maintenance."

You better not be lying to me. It's not right to break into your neighbor's house and steal.

"Are you a thief?"

"No," I work for the FBI

Oh you must be joking, no do you want to see my badge, lady you just made me laugh, I don't laugh enough.

"I would like to see your badge now, or is it fake?"

"It's no fake."

Let me open my fanny pack and show you. Here it is officer, it looks so official.

"How did you make it look so official?"

"I'm telling you the truth."

"Do you have a desk top computer?"

"No," I don't but my grandchildren do.

"Have you been to their house lately?"

"No," not for a week.

"How did you know my name officer?"

"You told me, and I still remember it"

"Ha officer are you trying to be funny with me?"

"No."

If you snoop around here, I'll have to give you a ticket. I haven't done any snooping around here. Yeah that's what they all say.

"Listen officer do you know how old I am?"

"No," and I don't really care

"What are you seventy-eight?"

"No," wrong, I'm eighty years old.

You don't look eighty to me, thank you for the compliment officer. You know what I'm thirsty for a spot of tea.

"Could you mind making me some?"

"Yes," but I'm not going to let you into my house.

"Why not?"

"Cat got your tongue?"

"No," it's my old husband

His attire is just a disgrace, he doesn't like police men coming in his house unannounced.

"Wait I thought this was your house?"

"No," he owns the house but it's still in my name.

"Are you always this politically correct?"

"Yes," and I know it's got to be getting on your nerves.

It seems to me like you are hiding something from me, no I would never do that. Don't say never Bernice. I'm a good man and I have kids of my own, I would never hurt a fly that was on your back.

"What does having kids having to do with anything?"

"It just means that I am a humble and gentle guy."

My great cousin has two kids and he's a real wild man let me tell you. Having kids doesn't slow him down one bit. Yeah so.

"What does he do for a living?"

"Last I checked he was a teller at the local bank, so he has it easy and can work banker's hours. I can sense that you are trying to make yourself appear to be a comedian, don't quit your day job."

You aren't funny at all, I really want to see the inside of your house.

"What for?"

"Just to see if you like to collect things."

I'm sorry but I don't think I should fulfill your want. The carpet is a mess, I haven't vacuumed it for three days. I usually vacuum the carpet every day for approximately one hour.

You must have the top of the line vacuum sweeper, no it's an old one from the fifties. I didn't know vacuums were around that long.

A man from across the street came walking over, hey officer I'm here to inform you that you're blocking my private driveway and you must leave. So officer get your bloody automobile out of here or else.

Chapter 11: Questions

I have been living here all my life officer and never saw a cop park in front of my driveway. So move your car now or I'll be back to start pushing it.

"Alright how about if I coast down the road further?"

"That would be fine."

I'm sorry I was rudely interrupted by this man, it's alright. Perhaps you should get going officer, no I'm not done with you yet.

"Officer why don't you get back on the road?"

"I'm a very sociable man and like to talk. Yes, I can see that."

"Do you have any rugs in your house?"

"Yes," I do

"Why must you know?"

"I was just curious that's all."

You just want to snoop around in my house. No, I just like to chat with nice friendly people like yourself.

"You seem kind pushy to me officer."

"So do people come over to your house often?"

"No," and that's how I like it.

"Do you live in a big family?"

"Yes, I do and I had enough with answering your questions officer.

It's going on eleven o clock. Alright officer I'll let you go in my house and I will make you a spot of tea.

"Do you have a favorite kind of tea?"

"No," I like any kind of tea.

"Do you like ice tea?"

"Yes," but I would rather drink hot tea.

I don't like drinking too much cold drinks. I like ice coffee. Now follow behind me officer, Bernice walked up the steps and tried to open the front door and it didn't open. The door was locked.

"What seems to be the problem?"

"My front door is locked"

"Where's your husband?"

"He's probably being lazy and watching the Telly."

He has irritated me all day. I'm sorry to hear that, Bernice tapped on the door, and waited a moment.

"What's your husband's name?"

"His name is Benson"

"Would you like me to go around back and get his attention?"

"No," I'm sure he heard me knocking on the door. Her husband came to the door, what do you want?"

"You must have accidentally locked the front door."

"Why's there a police officer standing by my door?"

"Him and I have been talking"

"Why are you letting him in my house?"

"He just wants a spot of tea and wanted to say hi to you."

Yeah and you want me to just believe that he is a friend.

"What has happened to you over these past few months?"

"I don't know dear, now I'm going to let him."

"Where Can I hang my coat?"

"Oh officer right here is a hook you can hang your coat on."

Now on your way out officer don't forget your coat, I'll try not to. You have a very nice house here. Thank you officer.

"What's your name officer?"

My name is Earl, it's nice to have met you

> "How long have you been a police man
> for?"

> "I have been an officer for three years now."

> "Have you seen any action while on duty?"

> "Yes," one time I was in a car chase for two
> hours.

> "I bet that was an adventure. Yes, and I
> don't like to drive."

> "Why not?"

> "I just don't trust the other drivers on the
> road."

> "Have you been in any bad car wrecks?"

> "Yes," I was in one.

> "What kind of car were you in?"

> "I was actually in my patrol car, oh that's
> lousy."

> "Did you have to pay for a new patrol car?"

> "No," the police department helped me to
> get another patrol car.

> "Are you making the tea?"

"Yes," I am, but it takes some time to get the water to boil.

I can't just snap my fingers and get everything done. So you'll just have to give me some time.

"What kind of tea are you making?"

"I'm making green tea"

"Is that okay with you?"

"Yes," that will be fine. I like your kitchen table, oh thank you.

The chair I'm sitting in is so comfortable

"Where did you get these chairs from?"

"Honestly I don't remember."

I love cuckoo clocks, and I see that you have one over there on the wall in your living room. You're very observant, then her husband walked into the kitchen.

Hey, yes dear, not to interrupt your conversation but we are out of orange juice, so I'm going to the store, I hope you behave yourself while I'm gone. Yes, I'll behave myself and so will Earl.

"Would you mind If I went over and took a closer look at the cuckoo clock?"

"No," I wouldn't, the tea should be ready soon, oh good Because I'm parched.

"Who made the cuckoo clock?"

"A wood worker, who is a family friend. It's good to have many friends."

"Would you like some lunch?"

"No," thank you, I'm going to go to McDonald's for lunch later.

"So you're a junk food junky?"

"You could say that."

"I don't like to cook either. The tea is ready and would you like anything else with the tea?"

"No," thanks

"What's with all the hanging plants in the corner of the kitchen?"

Oh I love to have plants in my house, they keep the air smelling good in here. I don't smell anything, that's alright must people don't.

"Do you know what kind of plants they are?"

"No," I just buy them and find out later what kind they are.

I like any kind of plant as long as it is in a hanging basket. You must have five hanging basket plants, they take up a lot of room in your kitchen.

"Yes," I know that and I don't like plants in my house.

"Why not"

"Because the only plants that I have are outside plants. As I look out the kitchen window I can see that you have a garden."

"How often do you tend to your garden?"

"Once every two weeks or so."

Those poor deprived plants in your garden, I bet if they could talk they would be crying out to you, now don't be so silly I wouldn't let anyone of them die. I'm glad that, I'm not a plant or I would be dead by now.

"Does your husband get you flowers?"

"He does only when he's happy with me and how often is that?"

"Let's just say he hasn't gotten me flowers in six months."

I'm sorry to hear that, but he seems like a good man for the short time that I saw him.

"Would you mind if I walked around your living room?"

"No," not until you finish your cup of tea.

I have a pet peeve about people walking around in my living room while sipping on their tea. Why's that, don't ask Earl. My great aunt had come over and she's always messing up my house.

One time I went away for three hours on a shopping spree and with my girlfriends. When I came back home all of my hanging plants were thrown away, there was a huge stain on my rug in my kitchen.

"What was her explanation for the stain on the rug?"

"She said that she had been brewing a cup of coffee, when she picked up the cup of coffee and it slipped out of her hand and went onto the floor. I was so furious with her and I couldn't forgive her for weeks afterwards."

"What was her excuse for the throwing away your hanging plants?"

She said to me that the bottom of the hanging pots were old and cracking and that every time that she would water them dirty black water would drain down onto the hardwood floor.

I couldn't even stand to look at her after that, I was more than angry with her. I was going to tell her to get out of my house, but my uncle told me not to.

"How long has it been since you have been on a Cruise for?"

"I've never been on a Cruise before."

"Would you like to?"

"No," cruses aren't for me, I get sea sick so easily.

My cousin actually has a huge bay liner, that he takes out to sea. He took me out to sea twice and both times I got so sea sick that my face turned blue.

The second time he took me out on the ocean the waves were so choppy and made the entire bay liner rock back forth. I was standing on the outer deck and one big rogue wave came along and rocked the boat.

Chapter 12: Situation

That day I was wearing a nice red leather pocket book, it slipped off of my left shoulder and fell into the water below.

"How did you get your pocket book back?"

"Luckily my cousin had a large net and with some luck and patience he was able to retrieve it for me."

Although my pocket book smelled like sea water for two weeks afterwards, I was able to find a way to get the ocean smell out of it. I used a smelly fragrance thing. I don't remember what it was, so I wouldn't want to go on a Cruise. Unless it's a Cruse that would take us to an island in the Bahamas. Actually there's a Cruse that's going to the Bahamas and it leaves in a month.

"Would you be interested?"

"No," I would have to speak to my husband about it, okay well let me know then.

I sure will, that tea you made me was just spectacular.

"Where do you get your tea bags from?"

"I get them from the local grocery store."

"What's the name of the grocery store?"

"It's called Hill crest grocery store."

"Do you shop there often?"

"No," the last time I had shopped there, let's just say I had an accident.

"What kind of accident?"

"I won't say, but I was so embarrassed that I hope it never happens again."

"What was so bad about it?"

"There was a lot of property Damage to say the least."

"What did you?"

"Alright fine I'll tell you."

"Was the tea that you gave me caffeinated?"

"Yes,"

"Oh no I'm going to have a problem."

"What kind of problem?"

I have a heart condition and now I feel like my poor heart is going to bust out of my chest.

"How's your heart feel now?"

"It feels like it's beating too fast."

"Do you feel light headed at all?"

"No," I can feel my heart racing.

"Do you have medicine with you for it?"

"Yes," and it's in the pocket of my coat.

Go get your coat and I'll tell you the rest of the story. Earl walked into the living and looked on the hanger for his coat and it wasn't there. Bernice we have a serious problem on our hands. What's that? Your husband took the wrong coat with him. Oh my heavens, what should we do? You are going to have to call an ambulance.

I've never called 999 before, you got to be kidding me, no I'm not Earl. I tell you what Bernice I will call 999 for you. I've called 101 before, for what? My cousin was chopping up carrots and cut his little finger. What did they say when they picked up? Well they said that they were the local police and that I should have called 999.

Where they mad at you? No they just told me who to call and hung up on me. Earl you don't look so good, your face is turning all white. Here why don't you lie down on my leather couch? I think I will do that. Would you like a pillow for your head? Yes, please, hold on I have to go up into my room, my husband won't be happy about this, because I am going to go get you his favorite pillow.

Bernice came back with a large blue down pillow. Oh that's just the pillow I was looking for, thanks so much.

"What's that running water sound?"

"I don't hear it, it's coming from up on the second floor."

It's probably the toilet again, I've had more problems with that toilet for going on two years now. Hurry up, I need the phone to call for help. I'm getting short on breath, oh dear your face is getting all red but your cheeks are still white. You kind of resemble Casper the ghost, oh please don't say that. Can't you just unplug the phone and bring it in here to me.

No, I can't do that and I don't have a cellar phone.
Okay let me get up again and go into the kitchen.
Earl could barely get himself up off of the couch.

"Do you need some help getting up?"

"No," I just have no energy and feel sick to
my stomach.

Take a seat here by the phone and dial the number
and I shall be back.

While Earl dialed the number, Bernice headed up
the stairs. Bernice slowly crept up the five steps and
then into her bathroom. When she got there, she
saw an immense mess.

The toilet bowl was leaking and there was water all
over the floor. She quickly opened the closet that
was nearby her bathroom and when she did a whole
bunch of towels fell on her and this made her fall
down onto her back.

She let out a groan and tried to get back up, she said
out loud oh my aching back. She got herself up
again and she shorted through all the white and red
towels.

She had three red towels and four white towels. The
one red towel had a stain on it. The stain looked like
it was red wine.

Oh my husband is such a slop and never puts the
towels away in a neat fashion, she thought to herself

I'm going to have to have a long talk with my husband when he gets back here.

She opened the bathroom door dreading what she might see, and there was still water all over the floor.

She took all the towels and threw them down on top of all the water, she was able to dry up some of the water but the floor still remained very slippery.

She was being cautious not to slip and fall. She walked over the towels and stepped over to the toilet bowl. The toilet was just clogged up. Water was still seeping out of the cracked toilet bowl.

This is driving me out of my bloody mind. She happened to look down the hallway and there was Corrine's cat. What are you doing here Mr. Mittens? You better get out of here. I bet Earl let you in, not knowing that you're not my cat.

Would you please stop looking at me Mr. Mittens? Can't you see I have a job to do here. Mr. Mittens walked closer and meowed. No you got it all wrong Mr. Mittens I'm not going to pet you so don't even think of it. Mr. Mittens remained standing in the doorway of the bathroom.

Oh you goofy cat, why must you always be staring at me? It really freaks me out. Yes, you have pretty green eyes, but I still don't like you because you're a cat.

Bernice went to walk over to the sink and slipped on the slippery floor and fell into the shower curtain, she was lucky that the shower curtain had caught her and lessoned her fall.

The shower curtain ripped in two places and fell down. Bernice was having difficulty getting herself up. She pushed on the side of the tub to get up.

Her right sleeve was soaked from the water that was still on the floor. Oh goodness now I'm going to have to throw this sweater in the laundry tomorrow. Bernice rolled up her right sleeve and went on with what she was doing. As she washed her hands a lot of water was collecting in the bottom of the sink. There seemed to be something wrong with the drain hole.

She tried to shove her hair brush into the hole to unclog it but it did nothing but make the problem worse.

Chapter 13: Hospital

Meanwhile Earl just got off of the phone. As he sat there he felt something on his face. He looked up and saw that there was water dripping from the ceiling.

He looked up and another drop came down and landed on his nose. So he got up and retreated into the living room. In his mind he thought to himself this house is beginning to fall apart and I don't like it.

He thought on, I hope that I can get out of this house soon. All of a sudden he heard a noise and he got up and looked out the window. There was an ambulance parked right outside. The lights were on but the sirens were not on. This seemed odd to Earl. Earl went to sit back down and his chest began to hurt. Two EMTs got out of the ambulance and brought out the stretcher, they walked up to the front door and knocked.

Hello, is there anyone home?

Earl quickly opened the front door and let them in. Hi sir, where;s the patient?

I'm actually the patient.

What seems to be the matter?

My heart beat keeps on jumping up then way down.

Okay sir, what's your name?

My name is Earl and how long have you
been having these symptoms?

The symptoms just began today after I drank
some caffeinated hot tea.

"So you're a police officer?"

"Yes," I am, and I love my job.

"Have you ever called 999 before?"

"No," I haven't.

I'm healthy man and this is the first time I was sick.

"Is this your house officer Earl?

"No," this is not my house; it belongs to a
grandmother whose name is Bernice.

"Are you just visiting with her?

"Yes," I am

"I'm going to ask you to get in the stretcher
right now."

I will, he slowly got into the stretcher, now I'm
going to strap you in. Let me know if the straps get
too tight, the straps feel just fine and thanks for
asking. We want to make sure that you're
comfortable, it's going to be a long ride.

"How long of a ride is it going to be?"

“If we leave now it should take us close to an hour until we arrive at the hospital.”

“Which hospital are you taking me to?”

“The Rosemont general hospital.”

They’re the best general hospital in the area, I wanted to say goodbye to Bernice. Now I’m going to put you on oxygen.

Is the oxygen tube comfortable in your nose?

Yes, it feels just fine.

“Would you like to sit up further or lay down in the stretcher?”

“I’m comfortable just the way that I’m laying.”

“How’s your heart feeling right now?”

“It’s feeling fine.”

Alright I’m going to load the stretcher into the ambulance now.

“Are you cold?”

“No,” I feel just fine thanks.

Cody is my partner here and he’s going to take your blood pressure while I’m driving to the hospital.

"How long have you been an EMT for
Cody?"

"I have been an EMT for two years and I
love every minute of it."

 I'm thirty years old and I have twin girls at home. I
was engaged for a few years and then she left me
for another guy. I'm sorry to hear that.

"How's your breathing?"

"My breathing is okay."

"How comes when you pulled up you only
had the lights on and the siren wasn't turned
on?"

"Because the sirens are loud and annoying,
and drive me crazy after a while."

But I thought it was a law that you had to have the
sirens on.

"No it's no law, who told you that?

"A friend of mine.

Well tell him that he is wrong.

"Have you lived in England all of your
life?"

"Yes," I have, I was born in Salisbury
hospital.

"Are your mother and father still around?"

"No," unfortunately they passed away three years ago.

"May I ask what happened to them?"

"It's a long drawn out story."

"How so?"

My mother and father contracted brain cancer and the cancer spread all over their brains and that led to their deaths.

For a while after their deaths I was so saddened and could not believe that cancer took my mom and dad from me. I know how you feel, my sister had breast cancer and she beat it once, but then it came back for a second time and she fought it with chemo therapy and did everything that she was supposed to do. Just two months later she was at home ready to go to sleep and well she collapsed onto the floor and that was the end of her.

"Who told you about what happened to her?"

"Her husband told me."

It was a week before Christmas and I felt so bad for my family. I want you to let know that this next part of highway is going to be particularly bumpy and tell him to hold on tight.

"Did you hear what he said?"

"Yes," I'll hang on good.

"Is Bernice going to come to the hospital
and visit you?"

I think she would, but she's not going to know
which Hospital that we are going to.

"Do you have her phone number?"

"No," I don't. Don't worry you won't be in
the hospital for long.

All of a sudden the ambulance went over a big
bump and threw everything around, including Cody.
Ouch my head just bounced off of the cabinet.

"Could you please slow down?"

"Yes," I will, but it's not going to help
much.

"How do you know that?"

"I don't know, but this particular stretch of
high way has always been bumpy for as long
as I have remembered."

"How fast are you going?"

"I'm going sixty-five miles per hour, and
I'm not going to slow down until we get to
the hospital. You're lucky that you aren't in

rush hour traffic. Listen guys I don't want to hear the both of you arguing."

"Can you both just do your jobs and get me to the hospital?"

"Yes," we can do that, take time later to discuss personal stuff.

I'm sorry; You better be sorry. Okay were five minutes away now from the hospital, thanks for letting me know Ricky.

You know this patient is the grumpiest patient that we had all day. Hey don't speak like that in front of me, wait until I'm out of here to start talking about me.

Chapter 14: Pests

Alright we have arrived at the hospital. So I'm going to unlatch the stretcher from the ambulance and take you straight into the emergency room.

"Are you still feeling alright?"

"Yes," I feel fine

"Is the oxygen set too high?"

"No," it feels just right to me.

"Why are you so grumpy all of a sudden?"

"I just don't like hospitals."

Cody walked over to the window where the head nurse was and said to her, here is the new arrival.

"What's his name?"

"His name is Earl and can he talk to me?"

"Yes," he can

"Can you pull his stretcher over here by my desk so that I can talk with him?"

"Hi Sir how are you doing today?"

"I'm doing okay so far, and you don't have to call me sir."

My name is nurse Scarlet and I'll help you today. That's just fine.

"What made you call 999?"

"It was because I thought that my heart was going to beat out of my chest."

"Are you trying to be funny with me?"

'No," that was one of my symptoms.

Would you do me a big favor and take off your officer hat. Us nurses don't like when people where hats in this hospital.

"That's kind of strange don't you think?"

"No," and I think you are strange.

"Would you let me put on your identification bracelet?"

'Yes, that would be okay."

"Are you going to put an IV into my arm?"

"Yes," and we are going to keep you over night. Oh no I can't be here that long, you'll be fine.

"Am I going to have to tie you down?"

"No, I'm terrified of needles."

Don't worry, I'm quick and I'm good at finding good veins. That still doesn't make me feel any better.

"Can't you just lie and say that you put an IV in my arm?"

"No," I can't

"Which arm would you like me to use? or doesn't it matter?"

"It doesn't matter which arm."

I got you all checked in.

Meanwhile back Bernice's place, Bernice was finally able to get the floor dry and then walked Down the steps back into the kitchen. Mr. Mittens followed behind her. Oh for heaven's sake Mr. Mittens please stop following me. I tell you what Mr. Mittens, how about if I let you outside for a while and please don't run away on me.

Bernice looked out the kitchen window and saw a small bird that was making a nest in the green hedges.

Bernice soon grew tired of watching the bird and went to walk into her living room and almost tripped over Mr. Mittens.

Come on Mr. Mittens you need to go outside for a while, like I said before you better not run away you silly cat.

Bernice opened the door and Mr. Mittens ran out like he was shot out of a cannon. Oh my what have I done, now Mr. Mittens will never comeback. She thought on how she was going to get the cat to come back.

She thought maybe I should bait him in somehow, then Bernice was thinking about what happened to Earl.

But the thought quickly left her head. She looked down at her wrist watch and it showed that it was two in the afternoon. She couldn't believe what time it was. She was so hungry for strawberry jelly.

She opened up her refrigerator and looked for a jar of jelly. She saw a jar of pickles and there was a carton of milk.

The cartoon of milk was right behind the large pickle jar. Her hands were slipperily and she knew that she was going to have to be careful.

She saw that there was a bag full of lettuce and behind the bag of lettuce was a jar, the jar was small and she knew that it might be what she's looking for.

She moved the bag of lettuce, and reached in and pulled out the jar of jelly. She took a good look at the jar and written on top of the jar, was strawberry jelly. She was so thankful to find a jar of strawberry jello.

All of a sudden the jar of jelly slipped out of her hands and broke when it hit the floor. Strawberry jelly went all over the floor, and made such a sticky mess. Bernice couldn't believe how she let the jar of jelly onto the floor.

Oh my Heavens, now I have made another mess. She thought to herself I'm such a clutch. She went back to the cleaning closet and grabbed the mop and bucket and cleaned the mess up.

It took her a good ten minutes to clean up the jelly mess. When she was all done she was out of breath and took a seat in her recliner.

She was still hungry for some strawberry jam, she thought to herself there must be more jam somewhere in the refrigerator. She happened to look down at the carpeting and saw there were three carpenter ants crawling along by her right foot.

Oh dear now there are ants in my house, I can't stand for this. Then a third ant came crawling along. Bernice stood up and let a moan and grabbed a Kleenex. She took the Kleenex and bent down and tried to catch the three ants but was just too slow and they crawled away.

She shouted out loud hey you ants get back here; I'm going to get you, you ants don't listen to me. She walked along at a faster pace and bent down again, oh my goodness I can barely bend down to touch my toes oh what a pity.

Then of the three ants crawled up on her shoe and continued to crawl up her left leg, oh dear god now I have ants in my pants.

Get out of my pants you crazy little creature, you don't belong on my leg you little pest. Bernice took her right hand and was able to get the ant. I got you, little pest. From now on you ants better leave me alone or else. I have enough to deal with anyway. Bernice walked over to her front door and opened the door.

Her jaw dropped when she looked out and saw who was standing by the door. It was Mr. Mittens, he had a mouse in his mouth.

All she could see was the mouse's tail hanging out of his mouth, she opened the door and Mr. Mittens ran in the open door. Then she shouted get back here with that dead mouse Mr. Mittens.

Chapter 15: Mr. Hinkle

Mr. Mittens ran into the other room and she could not seem to find him. Where are you Mr. Mittens? I'm not in the mood to play games with you.

I don't want that stinky dead mouse left in my house. I'm tired of chasing you all around my house. You have made me out of breath, I'm not happy about that at all. You have endless energy and I don't you silly cat.

"Mr. Mittens where are you?"

"Please come out Mr. Mittens, I don't have time for this."

"Why must you hide from me?"

Your such a disgrace Mr. Mittens. I can't believe how much time I have wasted looking around for you. I can't keep looking for you, besides that I have to check on the neighbor's house. Okay Mr. Mittens you can stay lost, I'll be back for you later, don't bring in anymore mice with you.

Bernice walked through her living room into the kitchen. As she walked along a drop of water came down from the living room ceiling, and went onto her forehead.

She looked up and another drop came down on her forehead. Oh my heavens now I have a leak, that's just great. Oh now I'm going to have to call the repairman. She walked into her kitchen and took a moment to think.

She had to think to herself where she had the repairman's number written down. It didn't come to her right away but she thought deeper into her mind.

Then it came to her, she walked over by the dishwasher and opened a drawer. In the drawer was an old crinkled piece of paper, she unfolded the piece of paper and the number was on it.

The repairman's name was Mr. Hinkle. So she took the piece of paper along with her and sat down by the phone in her kitchen.

She took the phone and twisted the dial to get a dial tone. Then she put in the number and the phone began to ring, it only rang twice and Mr. Hinkle, answered and said hello who is this? Oh hi Mr. Hinkle this is Bernice, Mr. Hinkle thought to himself oh lord not this lady again.

"What seems to be the matter?"

"I happened to walk through my living room and a drop of water came down from the ceiling."

I was just out there a month ago and you had so many more problems than what you mentioned to me.

Then you said to me that you were unhappy with how much I had to charge you. You're one tough women to work with.

"I know that, when would you like me to come out?"

"I would like if you could come out today in an hour."

That would be alright with me, I'll see you in an hour, oh and Mr. Hinkle there's a problem, and what is that?

"I can't find my cat; could you help me to find him when you come over?"

"No"

I'm not in charge of finding your pets for you. Come on please lend a hand in finding my cat. I tell you what if you pay me a little more when I come I'll look for you cat.

That's a deal, I'll see you soon Bernice. She hung up the phone and relaxed a moment and a thought came to her mind. I wonder if Mr. Hinkle is going to be nice or grumpy when he shows up. Then all of a sudden she smelled a real foul odor coming from the ceiling.

She stood up and walked over by the steps that led up to her bedroom. She could really smell the foul odor now.

She carefully walked up the steps and walked into her bedroom and the smell was lessoned by the good smelling candle in her room.

She walked around the corner and began to walk up the steps into the attic. The smell was so much worse up in the attic.

Once she got up into the attic, she began to look around. There were five cardboard boxes just thrown wherever.

Towards the left side of the attic. The smell didn't seem to go away at all but got even worse. There were two rugs in the middle of the attic, there was something hanging down from the attics ceiling. Whatever it was, it was all black and appeared to have little wings.

She came to the realization that it was a bat. Oh my goodness I never thought that I would have found a bat in my attic. Alright Mr. Bat don't give me a hard time catching you. I'm just an old grandma who isn't fast and is weak.

The bat never moved a muscle, it looked like it was dead. Then spoke out loud and said oh my lord it's so hard for me to even reach the bat.

I hope that I can reach you, you goofy bat. Bernice reached over using her left arm, and could barely even reach the bat.

She crawled along, till she was closer to the bat. Now I got you, oh my goodness you stink so bad. I think I'm going to hold my nose because you stink worse than a corpse.

I can't believe I forgot to put a pair of gloves on. I'm never going to forget again, to wear gloves. She saw that there was an old shopping bag by her left foot, and took it and placed the dead bat in it. I'm glad that I'm done with this job, she carefully crawled along over to the steps that lead down from the attic.

The steps were kind of shaky and this put her on edge. She held on for dear life and got down off of the last step and was now safe again.

She held the bag and the first trash can she saw she threw it into. Then she thought to herself Now I hope that I can, find the silly cat.

She took her time going down the steps into the living room. She was so out of breath that she had to sit down on the last step. Oh I'm so tired; I have been doing more work then I should be.

Soon she was able to catch her breath and walked back into the living room. Then she heard a knock at the door, she walked over by the door and swung it open, Mr. Hinkle was standing there right in front of her.

"Hey how are you?"

"I'm good, can I come in?"

"Yes," come on in.

Mr. Hinkle was wearing an old worn out baseball hat with the Mets emblem on the center of the hat.

He was wearing over hauls and a green shirt that had some grease stains on it. He was wearing black pants with a few rips in them.

"So how are you feeling today?"

"I feel alright, now"

"Could you please show me where you think the leak maybe?"

"Yes," let me lead you into the living room, she pointed to a particular place in the ceiling.

Chapter 16: Effort

Oh I see it right there, alright and I'm going to have to turn off your water for an hour or so.

"Is that okay with you?"

"Yes," that'll be okay.

"Now what about that cat?"

"It's funny that you ask me about the cat."

"Whose cat is it?"

"It's not even my cat."

What! I thought that it was your cat, then I don't feel like looking for the cat. I don't blame you, but it's important that I find the cat.

Listen, it's not funny and I'll fix this leak but it will take me two hours just to fix it. That's fine I'll leave you too it then.

"Oh and before would you like a spot of tea?"

"No," thanks I'm too focused on the job at hand here, but thanks anyway.

"May I ask where you are going in such a hurry?"

"No," you don't have to know everything about the life of a boring old grandma.

Your life is far from boring, you're more active than most eighty years old. Thanks for the nice compliment, you're welcome.

"Are you going to make dinner tonight?"

"Yes, "just for me, and no one else. I thought you had a husband, yes I do but he can fend for himself.

"That's kind of mean to say don't you think?"

"Yes," but now I have to go.

If you happen to see a white cat catch him and keep him in the room with you. Will do. Bye now.

Bernice quickly walked out the front door and walked towards her neighbor's house. It stopped raining and she saw her husband walking down the side walk and she quickly hid behind a tall green hedge so that he wouldn't see her.

He walked past the hedge and didn't even notice that she was there. He didn't watch where he was walking, and almost tripped over an uneven part of the side walk. Bernice chuckled and went on her way to her neighbor's house.

She watched as her husband opened the front door and entered the house. She heard some birds chirping, there was a young couple walking along the side walk.

The man was wearing a gray trench coat, the women was wearing a little white dress. She had a red flower tucked behind her left ear and had a gorgeous smile. Her husband wasn't smiling and wore a frown on his face.

He didn't even smile once the whole-time Bernice was looking over at him. They walked on and were soon out of sight of Bernice. Bernice got bored of watching the couple and walked away over towards the door of her neighbor's house.

Once at the door she, took out the key from her back pocket. She stuck the key in the lock of the door and quickly opened the door. Once inside she felt cold, the living room was dark and felt awfully damp.

She switched on the light in the living room and took a seat on the couch. Suddenly the light began to flicker, she thought to herself I wonder what Mr. Hinkle is doing? Then she thought about turning on the Telly.

She decided to stand up and take a look at the shelf of books that was situated in the back corner of the living room. The book shelf was packed so full of books, there was a layer of dust all over the books.

There were two thick books in the center of the book shelf. She took out one of the thick books and took a look at it. The front cover was a dark blue and the back of the book was gray.

The title of the book was gray's anatomy. She saw that there was a little piece of paper on the shelf where the book had been. On the piece of paper, it said my grocery list. Bernice took the piece of paper and, threw it into the trash can beside the book shelf.

The book shelf looked sturdy enough, but there was a slight crack in it. Bernice opened the book to page three hundred and on the page, there was a title. It said the anatomy of the human brain. This didn't interest her and she closed the book up and put it back on the shelf.

Then she picked up the second large book. The front of this book was a dark green, and the back of the book was black. The title of it was Biology, there was a picture of an Iguana on the cover of the book.

Bernice wasn't interested in reading about biology and put this book back on the shelf. Then a screw fell out of the shelf. This startled her and she leaned over and picked up the screw from the floor.

She looked up at the shelf and saw that there was some kind of insect crawling along, the very top of the shelf. She couldn't think of what kind of bug it was. She took a closer look and she realized what it was, it was a termite.

The termite crawled along slowly and didn't care that Bernice was staring at him. The termite continued to walk along the shelf until it was at the very edge of the shelf.

The termite fell down onto the floor and kept on moving along at a slow pace. Bernice watched as the termite walked over to the wall and went into a hole that was in the wall. She didn't see any other termites walking along.

This was a good thing, she got down on her hands and knees and crawled over to the hole in the wall. She looked in the whole and heard a loud buzzing sound, she couldn't see if anything was in the hole because it was too dark.

She saw that there was an old rusty screw that was lying in front of the hole in the wall. She took the nail and shoved it into the small hole in the wall. Now you're trapped you ugly bug. But

I'm sure that you have another way out. Then some pain flew into her back, she let out a moan. She said out loud oh I can't stand getting old, she tried to get back up but really struggled getting her knees to straighten.

She pushed on left hand corner of the couch and was able to get up. Her back was still aching, she couldn't get her back to straighten up.

She felt like she was crippled. She pulled her shoulders back and was able to straighten up her back. Oh, that feels much better, she decided that she wanted to check out what else was in the living room. Off to the right of the book shelf was a small end table.

The table had a nice white table cloth on it, on top of the cloth was an old record player. There was a layer of dust on top of it, there was a record in it. There was some dust on the top of the record and she couldn't read the label on the record.

She took her left pointer finger and took off some of the dust that was on top of the record. She uncovered an area on top of the record and read that it said The Kinks.

Bernice had never heard of the Kinks before. She looked in the back of the record player and noticed that it wasn't plugged and something had chewed on the wire.

The wire appeared to be eaten half through and some of the wires were exposed. Bernice was careful not to touch the wire, but accidentally let the wire brush up against her.

She was so curious about who the Kinks were, so without thinking she took the plug and plugged into a plug in the wall.

She received a little shock and it made her hair stand straight up. Oh, my heavens that was a bad shock, she happened to look in a mirror that was off to her left. She saw that her hair was all standing up and tried to make her hair go back down.

She was so scared to touch the wire again, but knew that it wasn't safe to keep the record machine plugged in. However still wanted to hear the song by the Kinks.

Chapter 17: It Begins

She listened for a moment and was hoping that she would hear something, but didn't and grew frustrated with the record player. She was still afraid that she was going to get shocked so she left the wire alone for some time.

Smoke began to come from the cord of the record machine. This caused her to panic. So, she quickly unplugged the record player and left it alone after that point.

Then her nose began to run and so she took a Kleenex out of her back pocket and wiped her nose a few times with it.

Oh, dear I'm feeling like I'm getting sick and all of sudden she felt a chill going down her spine. She thought to herself I'm lucky that I didn't get a worse shock than I did from that old record player.

When she was done blowing her nose she used the same Kleenex to clean off the top of the record player.

She looked down at the record on top of the record player and noticed that there was a slight crack in it. She thought to herself everything in this seems to have something wrong with it.

She was able to get all of the dust off of the top of the record player. She was feeling proud of herself, for getting the record player wiped down.

Sweat began to run down off of her forehead, but something just didn't feel right in the house. The temperature in the house must have been rising and she couldn't seem to find the thermostat.

She walked down the hallway towards the master bedroom, and looked at the wall off to her right and there was the thermostat.

She could barely read the numbers on the thermostat, but she squinted and could make out the number.

It said that it was eighty-one degrees in the house. She was uncertain what buttons to push on the thermostat to change the settings on the thermostat.

Meanwhile back at Bernice's house Mr. Hinkle and her husband were having a talk about what they during the day.

"Why are you here?"

"I'm here to fix a leak that your wife called me about?"

"I'm sure that I could fix the leak myself."

No, you can't, I'm almost done fixing the leak so I suggest that you keep your mouth shut.

"Are you a handy man?"

"I can be when I want to be"

"How often is that?"

"Oh, when I feel like I'm full of energy I'll take the time and fix up the house."

"Do you know how to fix a leaky sink?"

"Yes," I do, I have probably just as many skills that you have.

"No," I don't think so

I've been working as a house improvement worker ever since I was six years old. My dad would take me along with him to work while he would work on his customer's houses. Okay and would he work long hours, he didn't like to take weekends off and would sometimes work on holidays.

"How was your dad's health?"

"He was a very healthy man and would very rarely get a cold."

But one time he got a bad case of the coughs and he had to go see the Dr. he wasn't very happy about it.

My father wasn't a very patient man and did like to have to wait in the waiting room, of the hospital. He would moan and complain the whole time that he would have to wait.

I would just talk to my dad, he would settle down. My dad and I could always hold a good conversation with each other.

"Was your dad married?"

"No," and I'm glad he wasn't.

"Why not?"

"Oh, I just can't stand how women can act sometimes and I prefer to live a single life."

"How many times a day are you called out to fix people's houses?"

"Twice a day."

"Have you ever done three house calls in
one day?"

"Yes," I have

At my age I'm not going to over work my body or I
might get sick and lord knows if I get sick again I
may not be able to get healthy again.

Last time I got sick I was sick for three full days
and I never want to have to stay in bed for three
days again.

"Are you ever late to a job?"

"No," If I'm late I say I'm sorry, to my
customer.

"Have you ever had to go to the nearby
museum and fix anything there?"

"No," I haven't

The museum is a large building, I wouldn't be able
to walk from the entrance of the building to the far
back corner of the museum.

Why not, I have a bad left knee and sometimes it
gives out on me and then I fall. I'm sorry to hear
about your knee oh, it'll be okay.

"Do you have to stand up on ladders for
your job?"

"Yes," of course I have to, it's part of my
job.

"Do you carry the ladder with you everywhere you go?"

"Yes," I have to, when I'm called the people don't tell me what kind of job I'm going to be doing, that don't sound right to me.

"Why can't your customers tell you what they want to have done?"

"They do, but they don't tell me everything."

"Have you gotten paid well over the years?"

"Yes," and I don't like to talk about my pay and my expenses.

You seem like the kind of guy who likes to keep secrets to himself. A man with a low voice, said hello this is Aetta from the FBI.

"What are you calling about this time?"

"We have a new mission for you."

I hope it's somewhere tropical, not quite. You're going to Lithuania; I've never been there before. A treasure hunter called us and said two of his artifacts were missing since he woke up this morning. You'll have four weeks to find the artifacts, good luck. Wait a minute, yes.

“Is someone going to pick me up and take me to the airport?”

“Yes,” in one hour.

Chapter 18: Mission

You'll be having a different pilot this time, oh my I hope he's good. He was a fighter pilot for 2 years, so he's good.

Perhaps I should ask my husband what he thinks about all this. This is only about you; he doesn't need to know about it.

“Is your husband with you now?”

“No,” he's in the hospital.

"What did you do to him?"

"Nothing, he did it to himself."

I have another thing to tell you about, we're going to be giving you a gun.

"When are you going to do that?"

"Once you have arrived at the location."

"Can you tell me more about where I'll be staying?"

"I sure can"

You'll be staying at the treasure hunters mansion, on his property there are two vineyards. There are six outbuildings, and Roman architecture throughout.

He has a large car collection, including an Austin Martins vanquish, and many other cars. After the incident he's having a new security system put in.

"Does he have pets?"

"Yes."

Just don't give him a hard time, I won't. He does have a weird pastime; he likes to do goat yoga and sometimes dresses himself in odd customes. He likes to do those two things twice a week, that sounds interesting.

"Do you think he'll let me try it?"

"I'm sure he will."

You're not going there to play around and party. I hope that he has tea there, after lunch I like a spot of tea. I'm sure that he has all the tea that you want there, I hope you're done asking me questions.

"Do you know how long my flights going to be?"

"No," I don't know.

I hope that you enjoy your trip, I'll talk to you later by now. She quickly got up and went into her bedroom and began gathering her things.

After quite some time, she had gathered everything together. After that she did some cleaning, then took a break.

Then there was a knock at the door, she stood up and took her suitcase with her over to the door. She swung open the door, and there was a tall muscular man standing there.

Hello Ma'am," how are you?"

"I'm doing well thanks."

He opened the passenger door; you go ahead and get in and I'll load your luggage into the trunk. It took the gentleman unusually long to load the luggage.

She was about to get up and go check on him when he came back. I don't know what you have in that luggage but it's awfully heavy. It shouldn't take very long for us to get to the airport, I'm glad to hear that.

"What's been going on with you?"

"The same old things"

My husband is in the hospital, I knew that he'd end up there eventually. I know that you mind when I have my radio on, so I have it off just for you. The car in front of him suddenly slammed on its brakes, making them slam on there brakes.

"Did you have to stop that hard?"

"Yes," or I would have hit that guy.

The constant jolting is beginning to get to me, there's nothing more that I can do. The driver in front of us, just gave us the finger. I should give him a piece of my mind; I wouldn't do that.

"You're not carrying a gun are you?"

"I must certainly am."

Lady you're crazy, I don't remember you having a gun on you last time, that's because I didn't. There's no need for violence, it's just a little traffic.

"Why are we stopped?"

"Because of the guy in front of us."

"What are you doing over there?"

"I'm saying my prayers."

All I want to do is live long enough to get to the Airport. Stop with all that drama, it's not that bad. Then when they passed the driver in front of them, he opened fire on them. Get down, they quickly sped up and the driver stopped shooting at them.

"Are you all right?"

"Yes," I am.

"Now my car is all shot up."

"Are you sure that no one is after you?"

"Yes," I'm sure.

They finally came to the exit and got off the highway. I'm glad that were out of that mess, they went down a short road before arriving at the airport. I know that you're in a rush but wait until I'm parked to get out. After he parked she opened the door and got out and headed over to the entrance. He took her luggage out of the trunk and took it over to her.

Thanks for the ride, you're welcome. A strange man wearing sunglasses, looked over at her. She wasn't sure what to think, then he started walking her way.

There's no need to worry Ma'am, I'll be escorting you to your aircraft. I've never seen you before, that's because I'm one of the new recruits.

The pilot is just going over his checklist and will probably be ready soon. These private jets are so space age looking, I'm used to seeing the outdated kind. She carefully stepped up into the plane, don't worry about your luggage I'll have them load it for you. Enjoy your flight, and he walked away.

She carefully sat down, causing her holster to fall onto the floor. She quickly gathered the holster and her gun, just then one of the stewardesses got on the plane. You have such a worried look on your face, it's okay I'm just worried about my husband.

> "Would you like me to get you a beverage while I'm setting things up?"

> "Yes," please I'd like a water.

I figured that you were going to ask me for the soda, I quit drinking soda a long time ago.

Then the pilot got out of the cockpit and walked over to them. She handed Bernice a bottle of water.

> "How's everyone doing?"

> "We're doing good."

We're waiting for a couple; they should be here soon. The ski's are clear, there will be no delays for today's flight.

Thanks for taking the time to talk to us, it's my pleasure. He retreated back up into the cockpit, closing the door behind him. A few minutes later, the pilot came over the intercom. The couple were waiting for aren't coming, now we can be on our way.

Bernice was sitting by the window, taking in the sights of the runway. You sure are a quiet one, no not always.

"What are you drinking there?"

"Sparkling wine."

I haven't drank one of those in a while, alcohol helps me to relax. I should have introduced myself earlier, but my name is Anjanette. It's a delight to have met you, likewise.

I've been doing this job for two years now, and I can say that I thoroughly enjoy it. At the end of this month, I'm planning a vacation, I'm not sure yet where I want to go. I was planning for my boyfriend to go on vacation with me, but he left me.

Now I think about it it's just that he's gone, it just wasn't true love. Suddenly she pulled out her gun, please don't hurt me.

The pilot of this plane is one of my exes, and he must die because he stole from me. You should have settled this issue while you were on the ground. I know how to fly planes, so we'll be okay.

Don't you dare try to get the gun away from me, I've been working on this plot for a while, besides that you're just a weak grandma.

"What did he steal from you?"

"My cash and jewelry."

She knocked on the door to the cockpit. When he opened up the door, she hit him in the face with the gun. He then became delirious and was whining about his face. I'm not sorry for messing up your perfect complexion.

You probably thought that I forgot about what you had stolen from me, but you're dead wrong. I'm just trying to pilot this thing, just be quiet. I need something to wipe the blood off my face with.

You have always been such a whiner, just deal with it. You're going to scare the other woman on board, I don't care about that.

She might call the authorities on us, so what. Don't mess with that, I was just putting the plane in auto pilot.

She slapped him on his face, look at me. I want my jewelry back, and some money. We can talk about all that when we land, no stupid. I don't have your jewelry on this plane, I just have my wallet.

"Would you settle for a few $100 dollars?"

"No," I won't.

Then she began going through his pockets and found a small bag full of a white substance. You could've at least gave some of your drugs to me.

You know that I don't like to share my drugs, you're getting on my nerves. Now I know where that money of mine went to, you're so pathetic.

It's easy to figure out what else you were buying with that money. You have some hickies on your neck, you're such a bad person.

The world isn't going to miss you, I should go back out there and tell her everything that you've done. If you're looking for an apology, you're not going to get one.

He tried to punch her but she dodged his punch and kicked him in the face. He slammed her into the controls, you're not so tough now are you. While they were fighting, Bernice drew her gun pointing it towards the cockpit.

Suddenly both of them came out, don't shoot us. The woman's face was bloodied, the pilot had an angered look on his face.

The pilot tried to downplay it, by saying we were just having a disagreement. We had no idea you had a gun on you, we didn't know that grandmothers had the right to carry a gun.

I'm licensed to carry any gun I want, and you're not going to stop me. Don't shoot me, she attacked me.

You probably can't even see through the sights to hit anything. Oh, what a pity you are. Who gave you your gun, a nice gentleman at the gun store. He must have been insane to give you a gun.

You're just trying to get me wound up so I shoot one of you. You should put your glasses on so you can see, I can see fine without them.

You should go back to sleep and let us finish our argument. I'm not going anywhere; I'm standing my ground.

You have more wrinkles in your face than my grandpa who was 98 years old. You're wearing the stupidest looking outfit; nobody wears pearls anymore. You're just an immature child, who hasn't learned to respect his elders.

I have to get back to piloting the plane, bye granny. Bernice pulled back the trigger and fired at the girl who was pointing her gun at her. She fell to the floor, when he heard the gun go off he frantically ran out there.

"What did you do granny?"

"I killed her."

You didn't need to kill anyone, yes I did. She was a bad egg from the beginning, she couldn't pull the wool over my eyes.

You need to get off using those drugs, a politician friend of mine gave them to me. Then he's a crooked politician and needs to be ousted from power. But the ways things are I doubt anything is going to happen to him, but him and I go way back. I don't care how far back you've known each other.

You're going to have to help me throw her out of the plane, that's just appalling. I wish you wouldn't add comments to it. I feel terrible that she's dead, no you don't. Make sure that her wallet is with her, it's right here in her shirt pocket.

We're going to quickly open the door, after I check on the controls. I don't want us to crash while we're doing this.

You should throw away your gun, I'm not planning on doing that. The controls are okay, let's get to it. Are you sure we aren't going to be blown out too, I don't think so. Something tells me that you are high, not now.

I was high last night; my boss wouldn't let me get high on the job. Maybe if I was a politician they would let me, but my life depends on me being on my game.

It's true that I've been seeing a lot of women, I don't care about your personal life. You're just messing up your life, you don't take anything serious. They dragged her body over to the door, he pulled on the handle and the door opened. Her body was blown out of the aircraft, and fell down into the waters below, then they quickly closed it up.

I'd like to make a deal with you, I don't like the sound of this. Don't get yourself all tense, this has to deal with money.

Of course, everyone loves their money, and I'm sure you do deep down inside. I'll give you $65,000, to keep your mouth shut about this.

I'll have it wired into your bank account by the end of today. I just don't want this getting out, I don't want to waste away in prison. That would pay off some of my debt, it's yours then.

Just text me your bank information later. He handed her a little piece of paper, my number is on it 323-593-7740.

I have to get back to it, I have to call the tower to ask for permission for us to land. We can talk more when we land, she put her gun away and sat down.

Sometime later they landed, you know they're going to ask us what happened to the other passenger.

Tell them that we dropped her off in Houston. Since we aren't parked I'm turning off the jet, I'm sure you'll be escorted off the jet soon.

"Where you going from here?"

"That I'm not going to say, have a good rest of your day."

A gentleman escorted her off the plane, I hope that you had a good flight. It was just marvelous; the crew was just outstanding. They had all the champagne; anyone could have wanted.

The pilot was a fine young man, glad to hear it. She got in the passenger side, while the man finished loading up the suitcase in the back seat. He quickly returned and they drove off, I never expected you to pull out like you did.

That's because we're running late, we have 45 minutes to get there. She gripped her hands on to the car handle.

"Are you expecting us to crash or something?"

"No," I'm just getting ready.

You can put the pedal down if you'd like, okay.

"You're not much on conversation or are you?"

"No," Ma'am I'm not.

I think the owner of this place that you're going to see is crazy. Instead of guard dogs, he has two hyenas.

There's no way that could be legal, I hope that he has them locked away for my own safety. In the basement there are barrels of wine, among antique photographs that he collects.

Him and I used to be very close but aren't anymore. Eventually they came to his driveway, what an open area.

They drove down the driveway, came to the main house. He usually comes out when he sees a car coming.

"Will the hyenas be with him?"

"No," there are locked in another room.

"What's his name?"

"Aitzin."

"The minute that they parked the car, he came waltzing out."

"Is it safe to assume this is Bernice?"

"Yes," Sir it is.

Hello kind Sir, what a fine afternoon this is. The driver handed her luggage over to Aitzin. Let's get to why I called you in here, I've never had anyone steal from me. I can't figure out how they fooled my security system.

"Would you know about the time when they broke in?"

"No," I don't.

"Would you mind if I took a look around outside?"

"You sure can."

The driver told me that you have hyenas, yes that's true. You must spend thousands of dollars just to feed them, oh its quite a bit.

He took 2 keys out of pocket and handed them to her. These open up every door in my mansion, but don't open the door that's titled hyenas. I'll be in my office if you need anything.

Okay I will thanks. She took out her white gloves from her pants pocket, then went right to work looking for any possible clues around the yard.

Then began searching around the tall green bush's, one of the hedges was chopped down. She bent down and wiped away a thin layer of dirt, to her amazement there was a small wooden door with a lock on it.

The lock was open, she carefully opened it and found a golden key and put it in her pocket. Then she walked around back to the vineyard, there were strings of lights all around it.

At the top of the vineyard, was a nice charming red table, with chairs around it. Some yards away there was a tall post, with a camera situated on top of it. Then she spotted an out building, she couldn't quite make out what the sign on it said.

So she moseyed on down towards it, the cool breeze felt good. The sign said motorcycles in big lettering with a picture of a motorcycle on it.

She took out one of the keys that she was given, and pushed it into the lock. The door creeked as it opened, there were several fine restored motorcycles in there among some junk. She walked over to where all the junk was piled and took a quick look at everything.

When she went to step backwards, her foot bumped into the front tire of one of the motorcycles. She fell onto her back, and saw an old gasoline sign on the ceiling. She brushed herself off, she saw something in the exhaust pipe of one of the bikes.

It was a bar of gold, this astounded her. She thought to herself I better get out of here before I ruin something. She got out of there and locked up the out building.

There was an electric bicycle, lying down in the grass. She stood it back up, and pressed in the on switch.

Three small LED lights light up, and carefully got on it. She began peddling it, and was surprised by its speed.

Soon she came to the driveway, and kept going until she came to the road. Off to her left was a small gas station, there was a man sitting in a folding chair outside. There was a Landrover in the back of the place, she crossed the street over to the station. Hello Sir.

"What is it you need?"

"Nothing much, just to ask you a question."

"Did you see anyone go to the mansion at midnight the other night?"

"Yes," I did they were on motorcycles.

They were armed, so I left them alone.

"Are you an agent or something?"

"Yes," from the FBI.

You don't have to show me your badge I believe you. It was nice talking to you Sir but I'd better get moving, alright just be careful. She got back on the bike, and went down the road aways.

Off to her right was a dirt driveway, but there was no house that could be seen. She went down the road anyway, and stopped where the road ended.

She found it odd that there were two large rocks sitting beside one another. She moved the rocks, and wiped away some dirt and saw the outline of a metal hatch. Her phone was ringing, she answered it and it was Aitzin.

"How are things coming along?"

"Quite well."

I think that I've found something, I hope that you don't mind that I'm riding your electric bike. No that's alright, just enjoy it.

I'm going to come out there and see what you've
found. I'm going to bring some water along, you've
got to be thirsty by now.

"Whereabouts are you?"

"I'm past the gas station, at the end of the
dirt road."

I had a conversation with the man at the gas station,
he saw the perpetrators.

"Did he have much information to offer you
on them?"

"Yes," he did.

He said that there were two of them riding on
motorcycles, that's a good start.

"Did he happen to see their faces at all?"

"No."

He said that they were armed, I'm sure that they
were. He didn't tell me about the color of the
motorcycles, but atleast he told me something. I'm
going to hang up now with you, I'll be out there
shortly. After hanging up with him, she pulled out
the piece of paper from her pocket and texted the
pilot her banking information. He quickly texted her
back saying thank you.

She put her cell phone away, she turned around there was a walking dog robot behind her. I haven't done any karate in a while so I may be a little rusty.

You better not come any closer closer to me, or I'm going to karate chop you. The dog turned its head, you better be very afraid of me rover.

You know that it's rude to stare at people, just get out of here. She got into her karate stance and kicked it, knocking it over.

You're just an expensive pile of rubbish, now stay down. For good measures she kicked it again, get out of here you goofy.

I guess I must get you up, so that you can walk away. Lasers came out of it's eyes, before they hit her she stumped it's head to the ground. They're now you're dead, Aitzin soon arrived in his car.

> "Where did that robot come from next to you?"

> "I don't know."

I stopped it by doing some karate on it, it shot lasers at me.

> "Did it do anything else?"

> "Thankfully no."

I figured I'd bring some tools along with me just in case, he handed her a bottle of water. She took off the cap and took a sip out of the bottle.

"Can I please get in there?"

"Yes," you may.

This is a pretty gnarly lock, it may take us a while to pick. He set his toolbox down on the ground next to him. It's been a long time since I've picked any locks, you're talking like a criminal. You've all done things we shouldn't have.

I hope that we can finish this before nightfall, I'm sure that we will. He went back to his car and came back with a sledgehammer.

This should speed up the process, and hit the lock. After four blows with the sledgehammer, the lock cracked.

"What's that tool?"

"An explosive lock bomb."

He placeed it onto the lock, lit it and they quickly got back. They held their ears and it exploded, when they looked at the lock it was in pieces.

"How many of those things do you have?"

"I have 10 of them left."

She opened the hatch, and climbed down into the bunker. There are two ammo cans down here and a map of the area.

In the very back of the bunker is an assault rifle standing up in the corner. Maybe you should see if it's loaded, I don't want to check it.

Aitzin came down into the bunker, and began looking around. Bernice went over to the side wall of the bunker and noticed that part of the wall was inward slightly more than the other walls.

> "What in the world are you looking at over there?"

> "I'm looking at the wall."

I don't know what's so interesting about a wall, to a detective everything is interesting. To me you're just wasting time, believe me I'm not. She pushed on the wall, and it began to turn.

> "How did you know to do that?"

> "From past experiences."

The first place that I found a special wall was at a castle in Wales. That place gave me the creeps, I kept on looking over my shoulder.

There were a lot of bats in that place, I didn't dare go down to the dungeon. I heard something growling down there, to this day I'm not even sure what it was.

Perhaps it was a dog, there's no kind of dog that could have made this kind of growl. Now that I think about it, I think it was a lion.

"How many days were you investigating the castle for?"

"For a week."

That's a big room in there, I wonder what's in there. You can go in there first, Bernice stepped into the room. She happened to look down, and to her horror there was a tripwire.

She stepped back into the other room, there's a tripwire in there. I know what we can do for that, I'll be right back.

Some time later he returned, I figure that we can roll this bocci ball across the floor to set off the trip wire.

That's all well and good but if it's a big explosion we're going to be buried in here alive. I'm going back up to the surface, I don't trust it.

You can do what you want, he carefully rolled the bocci ball across the floor and it hit the tripwire and a small explosion ensued.

Bernice heard the explosion, and climbed back down into the bunker. She saw Aitzin, standing by a safe.

"Is everything alright with you?"

"Yes," it is.

"Have you tried to open it?"

"Yes," and it won't budge.

"Have you got one these open before?"

"Yes," I have.

We need to get this safe away from the wall, so that I can check the back of it. They were able to move it forward, and Bernice found a timer attached to it. The timer read 20 minutes, we have a big problem.

We have to disarm a bomb, I need your toolbox. He handed his toolbox over to her, she put it on the ground and began looking for the specific tools that she needed for the job.

She found the right tools, and began working at disarming the bomb. There were three wires, a red one, blue one and a yellow one. She cut the blue one, and the timer stopped. You did a great job at disarming the bomb, thanks. She went on to tackle getting the safe open, and began picking the lock.

After 45 minutes she was done picking the lock, and opened it revealing Aitzins stolen prized possessions.

I would have never found my things without you, plus you found my stuff in record time. After we get out of here, I'm going to call the authorities.

Together they packed up the toolbox and got out of the bunker.

Aitzin folded up the electric bike and placed it in the back seat, along with the toolbox. He opened the passenger side door for her, she got in.

Then they were headed back, if ever something is stolen from me again I know who to call. Once they got back, he quickly disappeared into another room.

He came back out with a drone, this is a spy drone. I have it set to look for every motorcycle 50-400 miles away from here. You certainly are very cunning with that thing, I wish you luck with it.

"How many pictures can that thing take?"

"30,000."

That's way over what I would have thought. It'll only look for sport bikes, that thing is very smart. Since you have completed the job so quickly you can just hang out here.

Then Bernice took out her phone and dialed her husband's phone number. He answered hello, I'm sure that you know who I am.

"How are they treating you there?"

"So far so good."

You called me at a good time, because I just got back from a barrage of tests. The doctor said that I'll be back home in two days, I'm glad to hear that. Aitzin put a glass of lemonade on the table beside her.

"How's your job going?"

"Very well I'm done with it."

That's the best thing that I've heard all day, the doctor is going to come in any minute so I have to go.

Thanks for the call, and I love you, I love you too bye now. Lemonade is such a delight to me, I haven't had it in ages.

Even my hyenas like it, they must be pretty sour themselves. If you were trying to make a funny there, it wasn't very funny. No I wasn't, and were going to change the subject.

Three days later she left, later that afternoon she got home and her husband was resting on the couch watching the telly.

Later in the evening the pilot wired the money into her bank account. The next day there was no more communication between them, he just mysteriously disappeared.

www.ingramcontent.com/pod-product-compliance
Lightning Source LLC
Chambersburg PA
CBHW061539120726
48001CB00004B/1631